NIGHT OF FIRE

As night approached, lightning began to flicker and fork; and after the sun had set in a sea of blood-red, the smoke cloud was lighted with deepening crimson, varied by vermilion and orange-yellow, while the rattling of thunder was in the air, and the floor beneath us continued to tremble. Not long after sunset, tormenting odors came to our nostrils, the suffocating reek of sulphur; and a gusty wind was thick with cinders.

Just then, from the skies above Clento Island, there came the most startling demonstration of all. The glowing cloud was split by a sword of white light. Blades of white and of eerie green and blue, began shooting in all directions; the whole prodigious crimson cloud puffed upward.

THE
ISLAND
PEOPLE

by

STANTON A. COBLENTZ

WILDSIDE PRESS

www.wildsidebooks.com

CONTENTS

CHAPTER I

COUNCILLOR OF THE WESTERN ISLES

" 'Small storms precede great! Small storms precede
great! Small storms precede great!' This was my only
word, Lampra, from the Seeress of the Dawn."

Her coppery hair bunched high above her shining
broad forehead, my fiancée stared at me with a puck-
ering of her small lips. Her little dark eyes stared past
me from the red sandstone balcony of her father's
house across the bay, where pleasure skiffs with tall
purple sails were skimming in the morning breeze.

"I had hoped, Klantor, she would tell more of your
future," Lampra answered wistfully, as she absently
fumbled at the sea-green robe that swirled about her
slender form.

I could not help smiling. I, Klantor Fey, youngest
and last appointed of the nine *Kolem* or Councillors

of the Western Isles of Atlantis, had no faith in the Seeress of the Dawn. But tradition said that every man, before marrying, must listen to her predictions at sunrise in the Cave of Blue Vapors at the base of Mt. Nublis. Only this morning, at Lampra's urging, I · had visited her.

"Now a fear comes to me, Klantor," Lampra burst out. "Your life—and mine—will be like the sea when the waves chop it into foam."

I laughed. The credulous creature had lived but nineteen summers and did not realize that seeresses also must have their daily fish and corn.

"Already your life has had its storms, Klantor," the girl pointed out, in her resonant voice. "As when the scientists of the Western Isles met here in Kallendra and picked you as their representative for the *Kolem*."

"That was but a little storm; some whitebeards complained that I was too young. But after all, Lampra, I've lived twenty-nine summers!"

"And you've made discoveries enough for twenty-nine lifetimes!" She spoke proudly.

She had, of course, exaggerated, though my work with the *bra* or super-telescope had added to our knowledge of the galaxies.

On an impulse, I hastily drew the girl to me; but released her when I heard a cough to my left and turned to stare into the chilly eyes of the old maid-servant Testa, who, with a robe like sackcloth about her skinny form, stood scanning me with scowling dis-approval.

Secretly cursing Testa, I glanced at the time-rod just inside my tunic and murmured under my breath, "Listen, precious one, I must not be late to my first meeting of the *Kolem*, at the Third Hour. But to-night—"

There was a dimpling smile on her perfectly formed features, a naive admiration. Surely, I was the most

8

fortunate man in all Atlantis to be betrothed to one so lovely, the daughter of the renowned and wealthy Argillon, second in seniority of all the Councillors of the Western Isles. At the time of the next full moon, we would celebrate our nuptials.

Why then was it that, as I slipped away down the sandstone steps to the irised seven-fountained court, the words of the Seeress of the Dawn kept ringing in my mind?—"Small storms precede great! Small storms precede great!" Of course, there was no sense in this at all.

Reaching the court, I paused to observe. Truly, our blue-skyed island of Xandu was the most beautiful of all the isles of Atlantis, and our capital Kallendra the fairest of its cities. To the north jutted the triangular cone of Mt. Nublis, dark green with forests. And to the south, the kindred peak of Mt. Jabavon rose enormous.

I strode along a walk rosy with oleander bloom, and soon, at the base of two great palm trees, I strapped on my *litto* or air glider, which consisted of two foot wheels, a motor fuelled by a liquid like alcohol, and a pair of aluminum wings tapering like eucalyptus leaves. On these I flew gracefully away.

But "flew" is not quite the word. While my wings rapidly beat the air, I glided a few feet above the ground, then shot briefly along the pavement on my foot wheels, before again gliding in air.

As I turned from a side avenue into the palm-lined main esplanade or *Cordocco*, I passed hundreds of fellow Kallendrans, all likewise traveling on *littos*. Their tunics and flowing wide-sleeved robes were of azure, purple, orange, scarlet, and snow white; and their *littos* were likewise of all hues.

But my mind was not on such spectacles. I was thinking how strange it was that I, Klantor Fey, should attend a secret meeting of the *Kolem*, the rul-

9

ing power of the Western Isles. True, the triumvirs or *Thadros* were the theoretical leaders; but these retained no more than a few judicial and appointive functions.

The *Kolem*, picked for nine-year renewable terms, were selected by the nine professional guilds. Only by accident, I thought, had the astronomers chosen me for the *Kolem*, not so much for my own accomplishments as because of the outcry that the *Kolem* had been monopolized by the gray-haired.

The great honor had come to me so recently that I had thus far enjoyed it in name only. But I had gritted my teeth and sworn by the nine gods of Mt. Nublis that I would serve well. Ah, how little I could see ahead!

At last I halted before the *Kolemna* or *Hall of the Kolem*, and left my *litto* in charge of an attendant. The building, fronting on a public park, had a bronze dome, surmounted by the image of a white sea gull. Pale green cacti surrounded it; three huge black wolf-dogs sat with their keeper before the main entrance.

However, the animals only yawned as I approached; and their master, an old man with a crooked smile and a bright red official tunic, blinked knowingly when I slipped a copper into his palm before he pressed a wall button.

Inside, a guard ushered me to the robing room, where for the first time I put on the official costume of the *Kolem*, a heavy gown of rippling gray-green, with a triangular gray-green headpiece.

Following the guard, I soon reached the Golden Conclave Hall, whose flame-colored light strips cast a fiery illumination from the walls and ceiling. The room was far larger than today's purposes required; six or eight hundred seats, arranged in a semicircle on the sloping floor, were intended for public meetings of the *Kolem*.

The hall itself was impressive. The front was marked by bronze busts of great past leaders; along the walls, and dangling from the arched, black marble ceiling, were images of war machines, featuring the mighty *thungsibgia*—great coils of wire capable of aiming fireballs from island to island. Over the main door, characters of flame stood out in the twenty-nine-lettered alphabet of Atlantis: *Light, Liberty, and Learning.*

To my surprise, only one of the *Kolem* had preceded me to the Golden Conclave Hall: a broad-shouldered gray giant who sat hunched forward in a front seat, reading a book through a pair of *changus* or magnifying spectacles.

I approached him and bowed far forward. "May the gods forgive me, Great One, for intruding. I am a new member, and may be too early."

He removed the *changus,* and cast me a long appraising stare out of his hard brown agates of eyes. The down-turning lips, the square jaws, the seamed and soured face, the mustache trained upward to two thin twirling points—this was the famous Wauglan Waud, Lord Magistrate of the Armed Defenders, and their representative in the *Kolem.*

"You are not too early," he growled, in a voice that scraped like filed metal squeaking over glass. It seemed to me that his sharp, cold gaze took in my every feature—my flowing auburn hair, the very shape of my domed head, the complexion of my bright blue eyes.

Without another word, he readjusted his *changus,* and returned to his book.

A bit taken aback, I sat down to await the other members.

But when they did come, I did not feel much better. They were all old, grizzled or white haired, or completely bald, not one of them too young to be my father. Their contemptuous sidelong glances made it easy to see that they resented the intruder from another generation.

I was feeling like a hare at a meeting of foxes by the time the last of them stalked in—Argillon, Lampra's father, the representative of the *Hassessi*, or lawyers. He came to me, took me by the hand, and introduced me to the others. But even he, with his clipped phrases, cold pale blue eyes, and long pointed intellectual face, seemed chillier than a knife blade.

"I understand, Klantor," he said, "something important is coming up today. Something extraordinarily important. Do not forget that a new member must arm himself with humility."

A hot flame shot through me. My disposition had always been fiery and independent; I would permit no clamps about my wrists.

It may have been fortunate that Drandro-dra, the representative of the *Fructra* or Church, saw fit just then to open the meeting.

CHAPTER II

IN THE GOLDEN CONCLAVE HALL

Drandro-dra was a swaying, withered fiber of a man, whose tongue seemed to move on rubber hinges. His mouth—a wide slit in his short, gray old face—opened in a slanted grin, revealing the metallic glitter of teeth capped with an aluminum alloy. His ears stuck out from a head with only the faintest remembrances of grizzled hair; his eyes were like pewter; the Adam's apple on his birdlike neck was working as he intoned the opening prayer, after a foot lever had sent a panel clattering open on the wall to his left.

In a niche, two figures in black basalt stood revealed: One, the image of a man, had the wings of an eagle, the face of a tiger, and a headgear of coiling snakes; the other was a woman with talons like a bird of prey.

13

Before these figures Drandro-dra prostrated himself almost to the floor.

"O Ablum! O Quag-ulta! God and goddess of the earth and heavens!" droned the priest. "Once more we place ourselves in your power! Once more we beg your blessings for your children of the Western Isles!"

As these phrases came forth, full-mouthed but hollow-sounding, I wondered how much faith Drandro-dra had in his own words. Here, in the world's most scientific age, the old superstitions were still on our lips.

With a sigh, Drandro-dra turned from the idols. His pewter eyes were fixed upon me, where I sat at the foot of a pale rose table; again I heard his voice, insidious and insinuating.

"My brothers of the *Kolem!* Today we welcome a new member. Will he not show us his credentials?"

I saw all eyes upon me—hard eyes, cold eyes, eyes inquisitive and cruel. Nevertheless, I strode forward resolutely, and after a bow, put a little blue-capped scroll in Drandro-dra's hands.

He gazed at it as if not already familiar with its contents, then solemnly announced, "It is well. Are you ready, Klantor Fey, to take the triple oath?"

"I am ready."

"First, the Oath of Fidelity. You must swear to respect the sacred laws and traditions of the *Kolem.*"

"By my reverence for Ablum and Quag-ulta, I swear it!"

"Next, as you venerate the gods, the Oath of Fidelity. You must swear to keep the good of the Western Isles uppermost in all your thoughts and deeds."

I touched my head to the image of the god and the goddess, and took my oath.

"Finally," Drandro-dra went on, with an ominous intonation, "the Oath of Secrecy. What transpires at our closed meetings must never be divulged. Never!

14

Under penalty of the vengeance of the gods!"

For a moment, I hesitated. In the very act of joining the governing body, I was expected to swear away my freedom of speech!

"Is it, respected Drandro-dra, is this necessary?"

A scowl crossed the wrinkled brow of the head of the *Fructra*. Frowns darkened the brows of the other dignitaries.

"It is not for a new member to question!" growled Drandro-dra. "If you wish not to utter the oath, doubtless the *Nuftt* will find some other representative."

"Be it as you say," I capitulated.

After I had taken the oath, Drandro-dra intoned another prayer, then mumbled, "Klantor Fey is now one of the *Kolem*," and turned to me severely.

"Klantor Fey! You have sworn to respect the holy traditions of the *Kolem*. One of them is that the young shall hear their elders with reverence. They shall not lift their voices, nor invoke their will against the elders, nor be heard at all unless from absolute necessity. This is important in the interests of harmony. For the law prescribes that all measures of the *Kolem* must be unanimous. Newcomers must defer to the old."

"Most honored Drandro-dra," I demanded, "was I not delegated as the full representative of the *Nuftt*?"

The members had shot forward in their seats, surprised disapproval in their cynical old eyes.

"True," Drandro-dra grumbled, half beneath his breath.

"Have I not then the right—the duty—to act as their full representative?"

"'Silence is often the speech of sages,' as the seer Tirrtho said long ago," quoted Drandro-dra, with a snort. "For a new member, you talk too much. But we must get on."

He paused. During the brief speechless halt, all eyes were fixed upon the appointee of the *Strenziz*, or Armed Defenders.

Wauglan Waud shot to his feet. I noticed again his square jaw and forceful manner, and his chest covered with shiny platinum decorations, as befitted the victor in the dread conflict concluded fifteen years before with the four Eastern Isles.

For a moment, Waud stood staring about the hall as at a field of conquest. Then, in his scraping, scratching tones, he began to speak.

"My brothers, you know that no man is more devoted than I to our beloved Western Isles. My life has been given to its safety, its defense. But the bitter fact is that we have never been safe. The ancient enmity between the Western and Eastern Isles, which has caused twenty-five wars in five hundred years, remains as keen as ever."

The speaker paused, and ground his teeth together.

"We cannot trust the Eastern Isles, nor negotiate with them. Knowing that they plot our destruction, we must have faith in nothing but our own right hands. We must exterminate them before they exterminate us!"

Waud's jaws came together with a crunch.

"This is all familiar to you," he rushed on. "Now for a new proposal, which, my brothers, you will greet with open arms: What we need is a secret weapon which the tigers of the East cannot answer."

His head swung to one side. One thin twirling point of his mustache was upturned defiantly; his teeth dug into his lower lip. His voice was lowered as he drew from under the table a map of the Nine Isles, which he unfolded before us. "Note this, my brothers!" He indicated, running the knobby fingers of one hand across the paper. "Not one of these islands is not of volcanic origin. In Klatchen, the leading isle of the

16

East, there are four volcanoes. Now here, my brothers, is a source of energy beyond our fondest dreams!"

During the charged silence that followed, we all shot forward in our seats. My head was so tilted that my headgear seemed about to slip off.

Strange then that I, of all the members, was the one to find words.

"Then you mean, respected Wauglan Waud, you mean to cause volcanic eruptions?"

He let the breath out with a hiss from between his half-closed lips.

"I mean just what you heard. I do intend to cause eruptions, by which the aggressor islands will be chastised as they deserve!"

"But how, honorable Wauglan Waud? How will that be possible?" demanded the high-pitched voice of Dr. Zuno Klan, the octogenarian appointee of the Guild of Physicians and Biologists. "To tamper with the powers of nature is not always easy, nor safe."

"To make war is not always easy, nor safe!" snorted the chief of the Armed Defenders. "But here, I have the papers! Everything has been worked out by our Super-Secrecy scientists. I myself can give you only a general idea. That is, if you wish it!"

"Yes, yes, yes, by the gods!" came an eager chorus.

I writhed and terror clutched at me.

"As I understand it, here's the situation," Waud related, swinging his arms like an orchestra conductor. "There are great ducts and cavities in the earth leading to the craters of volcanoes. These ducts or cavities are filled with overheated matter or magma, which sometimes erupts. Now here, as I have said, is a vast reservoir of hidden energy. The problem is to tap it."

"And can that be done, estimable Wauglan Waud?" asked Yuntu Ghratt, the pudgy, double-chinned representative of the Merchants, Bankers, and Manufacturers.

"Certainly!" Waud's fist came down decisively. "All we have to do is bore a secret tunnel under the sea toward one of the volcanoes of the Eastern Isles. Our geologists will chart the location close to overheated veins of magma. Suddenly we will let seawater into the tunnel. Its approach to the magma will heat it to boiling, producing great quantities of steam, which will turn the tunnel into an overheated boiler without an escape valve."

"So it would explode!" muttered Dr. Zuno Klan.

"And it would tear the thin crust off the earth above and break down the walls between it and the seething magma, into which seawater would pour causing still more powerful explosions as this turned to steam. Furthermore, the magma, released from the great pressure of its pent-up pockets, would join the steam in volcanic eruptions on a magnificent scale!"

Waud daubed at his eyes, which gleamed like a panther's.

"So the people of the Eastern Isles," he finished, in a screech, "would never menace us again!"

Again I found myself speaking—almost as if some power outside me had control of my tongue.

"Honored brothers of the *Kolem!*" I began, springing to my feet. "Consider what this might mean. Molten lava rolling over hills and plains, burning up every living thing! Explosions killing hundreds of thousands! Clouds of hot steam and dust suffocating and burning all who inhaled even a breath! Men, women, and children—the aged, mothers, babes in arms—all dying in agony! Is that how we, civilized Western Islanders, propose to wage war?"

As I sank into my chair, I was still shaken by my fury.

But from about me, all that I saw were cold, unsympathetic eyes. Waud's reply vibrated with contempt.

"I take it, my brothers, that we are practical men, not sentimentalists."

There were nods of agreement.

"But would your proposal, illustrious Wauglan, not involve great expense?" asked Yuntu Ghratt.

"Expense?" sniffed Waud. "What is expense, beside protection of our country?"

"Also," took up Argillon, a glacial glint in his calculating blue eyes, "there will be ways of financing it. There always are. The head-tax can be increased. The people will complain. They always do. But they will end by praising our leadership."

Foxlike smiles flitted across several faces. But a question was on the oily lips of Drandro-dra.

"Esteemed Wauglan, how to be sure that the enemy will not get wind of our plans and attempt a similar defense?"

Wauglan took a stride forward; a sneer wrinkled his arrogant lips.

"You overestimate those donkeys of the East! Our plans will be sealed tight! Each worker will know his own part, and none will be able to put the puzzle together."

"One thing you have not mentioned, revered Wauglan Waud," rejoined Dr. Zuno Klan. "In science there is no such thing as an exclusive idea. The Eastern Islanders may arrive independently at the same results."

"All the more reason we should not lag behind!" stormed Wauglan Waud, his voice grating like sandpaper. But just then I heard the slow, shaky tones of old Velto Vanrr, the white-haired representative of the *Clotilla*, or Association of Scholars.

"From all that I have heard, exalted Wauglan Waud, your scheme is a matter of theory only. Before we invest billions, how can we be sure it will work?"

"A good question!" acknowledged Waud. "That's the very thing I'm here to present to you today. All

19

that I want now is the authority to make a certain experiment and a vote of the necessary funds. A hundred million *Atlantids* will do for a start."

There was a pause. A groan came from Yuntu Ghratt. "A hundred million *Atlantids*," he pointed out, "is enough to build twenty *litto* factories."

Again the Lord Defender unfolded a map. "Here," he designated, pointing to a rippling jade-green patch, "you see these two spots of land, the Cocoanut Islands."

We nodded. Who had not heard of the idyllic islands?

"Fortunately," Waud rushed on, his eyes narrowing, "we have a mandate to rule them. Fortunately, also, they are volcanic. Fortunately, again, the smaller island, Hilos, is separated from the larger, Zuttel, by a channel narrow enough at one point for a doughty swimmer to cross. Therefore we can work from Hilos, drive an experimental underwater tunnel toward the active volcanoes of Zuttel, and cause an eruption. After this, Zuttel will be a nursery for the fishes."

For a moment I sat stunned, then was once more on my feet.

"But you cannot mean it, respected Wauglan Waud! The whole beautiful island of Zuttel—a sunny green paradise—to be blown to extinction!"

Waud looked past rather than at me.

"As I have said," he argued, with a particularly disagreeable squeak, "we are practical men, not sentimentalists. Esthetic values cannot be recognized in law or war. We must confine ourselves to the realities!"

Fresh fury was flaming within me.

"Is it sentimental," I demanded, "to ask: what of the people of Zuttel? Must they be blown into the sea, along with their island home?"

20

With a rasping laugh, the Lord Defender waved aside my question.

"People of Zuttel? Phew! Why, there are only a few thousand of them. Mere savages—of no use to anyone. Of course, being a humane people we'll provide for them—have them relocated."

"Surely, there are others," I pleaded, "who are with me in not wishing to destroy a fair and peaceful island."

A weighted silence followed. Then, after a long moment, I heard Velto Vanrr's thin, shaky voice. "I—I find it hard, respected Wauglan Waud, to believe in progress through volcanic action."

"I feel so too," chimed in Tellin Trus, the representative of the *Vrontal,* or League of Artists and Literary Men. "I am devoted to the defense of our country, but by the gods! there must be other ways than by making ash-heaps of picturesque islands!"

"There is no other way—not if we want protection!" denied Waud, his lips curling nastily. "So we have not one sentimentalist, but three! Ah, well, I will not press for a vote today. After five sunrises, we meet again. Meanwhile, you will have time to reconsider."

As the meeting drew to a close, I felt a fierce surge of triumph. For the present, at least, I had blocked Wauglan Waud's atrocious plan.

However, I did not like the frigid reproving look in the icy blue eyes of the man I most wished to please: Argillon, the father of my beloved Lampra.

CHAPTER III

FORBIDDEN RENDEZVOUS

A presentiment had come over me as I drove my *litto* down the palm-lined esplanade. Sunset was still an hour away when I dismounted and rushed on foot through the hibiscus-lined walks of Argillon's private estate.

I climbed the mansion's sandstone steps three at a time, crossed the wide verandah, pulled down the bronze clapper before a broad door likewise of bronze. This was the usual time for my rendezvous with Lampra.

Many seconds passed, and there was no response. I pulled down the clapper again; the metallic clang rang out hollow and ominous-sounding. A third time, and my uneasiness deepened to anxiety; a fourth, and I did hear footsteps within, but slow and dragging.

22

Then, with a jerk, the door had opened the width of a head.

"What do you want?" a grating voice shot at me, as the maid-servant Testa stood partly revealed in her robe like sackcloth, her thin lower lip curling.

"I—I want to see Lampra," I stammered. "We— we've an appointment."

"Lampra cannot see you!"

"I *must* see her! Let me in, Testa! You know I've always been admitted."

"That's none of my affair! This time you're not admitted. I don't disobey instructions for any cocky young fledgling! Now get out!"

A thin cackling laugh was followed by the thud of a door.

As I turned slowly away, my mind was already wrestling with the problem. What had I done to antagonize Lampra? But no! it was not she! Only this morning, she had been her warm, fond self. Then was this a plot of Testa's? The old hag, I knew, had always been jealous. Or could it be that Lampra's father was using my love to force my vote on the vital issue before the *Kolem?* But this was monstrous! Nevertheless, I could not forget his cold, disapproving eyes at the meeting.

As I dragged my way out into the garden, a voice rang merrily in my ears. "Well, Councillor, it's an evening such as only the gods could make!"

I looked down and saw the old gardener Ru Manir stooped above some small potted plant, his tanned face grinning from beneath his broadbrimmed grass hat.

Slowly he unbent his limbs and, waving a trowel, rose to a goodly height.

"For me, Ru," I answered, unable to keep back my feelings, "it's an evening such as only the devils could make."

23

He said nothing, but I did not miss the question in his glance.

"Listen, Ru," I confided, an idea coming to me. "I'm in a predicament. You know I'm betrothed to Lampra—"

"Yes, and a gentler dove never was in all the Nine Isles," acknowledged Ru, beaming. "You are blessed by the gods, Councillor."

"Not so blessed as you think!" Sadly I mentioned how Testa had barred me from the house.

"If I could only get a message to Lampra, without that she-goblin intercepting it," I hurried on, "things might yet come out right."

He glanced down at his potted plants, his old lips twisting with a wily smile.

"The gods are with you, Councillor. It happens that Mistress Lampra has expressed a desire for this pretty rose-azalea. Now a small note at the roots of the plant, with a few dead leaves covering it—"

I snapped a notebook and writing stick out of my tunic pocket, scribbled a few lines, and passed the sheet to Ru, along with two or three coppers.

An hour later, I was pacing uneasily beside a bamboo thicket near a trickling stream in the rear of Argillon's estate. Here Lampra and I had often had a rendezvous; and here I awaited her, in the desperate hope that Ru had delivered my message.

It was almost dark when I heard her light footsteps approaching. She gave a low gasp—and we were in each other's arms.

"O Klantor! Klantor!" she wailed, when at last she had disengaged herself. "I thought I'd never see you anymore—never! They—they forbade me!"

Even as I tried to console her, I begged her to keep her voice down, lest we be overheard. For safety's sake, I drew her into a recess of the bamboo.

"Who—who, priceless one, forbade you to see me?"

24

"*They! Father!* And his nasty old watchdog, Testa! He came home today, blazing angry. He said you'd done something very wrong. He said—he said, unless you changed soon, you were not the man for me!" .

I had jerked away from her; a stirring in the brush had alarmed me. But it was only a shuffling big dog.

"As I respect our love, I've done nothing wrong, Lampra. What did your father say my crime was?"

"He wouldn't say. It was a secret he had sworn not to reveal."

"I too, Lampra, have sworn not to divulge the secret. But if you have faith in me—if you believe in me—be sure that I was only trying to stop a vile outrage."

"I believe in you! I always will!" And again we were in each other's arms. But only for one moment. Just then, from the dusky path, we heard footsteps!

"It's that ogre Testa!" Lampra gasped, throwing one hand across her panting chest. "Quick! I must go, Klantor! Tomorrow, at the same time—if I can!"

Like a wild thing, she fled. From around a turn in the path, I heard a thin, harsh voice, unpleasant as the snapping of a whip. "Ah, here you are! A nice seemly thing for a tender chick like you to go out alone in the dark! Your father—"

The voice grew indistinct; faded into the distance. And I, stealing along a shadowy side path toward a rear entrance, seemed to hear once more the words of the Seeress of the Dawn, "Small storms precede great! Small storms precede great! Small storms precede great!"

During the next day, I fiercely planned my course. On meeting Lampra that evening, I would insist that she flee with me at once—I was making all the preparations. One of the *Ablio,* priests of Ablum, would

25

intone the marriage ceremony in return for the usual fee—and then let Argillon rage!

In the early dusk, I entered her father's grounds through a servants' back gate. Trembling, I took the path toward the bamboo clump. Would Lampra be awaiting me? I had almost reached the spot when, out of the shadowy foliage, a figure sprang up. My heart gave a leap; what I saw was not a beloved small feminine shape.

"Ah, Councillor!" came to me in a husky voice. "I was told you were coming. Here is a little plant, which the mistress thought you would like to see."

With a grim smile, Ru Manir was holding out a small pot containing a white azalea.

I seized the plant, brushed some dead leaves off its roots, and drew out—a scrap of paper! Then, straining my eyes in the fading light, I made out the words:

Dearest Love: I cannot keep our appointment. I am guarded on every side—followed everywhere. Except for Ru Manir—thanks to the gods, he is not suspected—I couldn't get even this to you. It will be useless, just now, to try to see you. I'm afraid to write more. But I will be loyal to you always! Sometime we will be united again. And now—farewell!"

The message was signed not with Lampra's name, but with a little symbol we had agreed upon for greater secrecy: "X * * * X."

With one hand, I clasped the message to my breast; after a mumbled word to Ru Manir, I wheeled about and, still clutching the azalea, staggered away.

CHAPTER IV

INVADING THE ENEMY'S STRONGHOLD

After a sleepless night, a reckless resolve had come to me. I must invade the enemy's stronghold, meet him face to face, and demand the reason for his hostility.

But would Argillon see me? Of course, I could not visit him at his home, where the way would be blocked by that she-buzzard Testa. Hence I hastened to his office in the huge granite building of the Guild of *Hassessi* or lawyers; and there I waited for two hours.

"Ah, Klantor! I've been expecting you!" he flung his greeting, as I entered a large elliptical room with a translucent pale blue ceiling. He was seated on an azure, cushioned divan, beside a pile of palm-sized

27

books, which could be read only with the *changus*, or magnifying spectacles.

As I drew near, I saw him much more clearly than at the meeting of the *Kolem*, and was shocked to notice how pale he looked, how blue his lips were, and how pinched his long, thin, coldly intellectual features seemed.

"Be seated, Klantor!" he invited, pointing to a pile of silver-embroidered cushions. "Yes, I've been expecting you."

"By the gods, how so?"

"Mere deductive reasoning, friend Klantor." He leaned toward me, and one thin bluish hand fondled his dagger-pointed gray beard. "You and I are both practical men, so let us go straight to the facts. You hope to marry Lampra?"

"Do I have to tell you that?"

"Very well. On general principles, I have no objections. You are well-built, able, intelligent. If you keep your wits, you have a future. But if your wits get away from you, your future will be an abyss."

"Just what do you mean, Argillon?" I asked, leaping out of my seat.

"Now, now, as you love our native Xandu, keep a rein on your emotions!" he counselled, still with imperturbable calm. "Let me explain. You, a novice, having won the rare honor of an appointment to the *Kolem*, have had the poor judgment to oppose its leaders at your first session. Now don't flare up again —I'm not saying you're not right in principle. But I've seen enough of politics, my young friend, to know that the man who is right in principle is too often crushed in practice. That's why I suggest a change of direction on this. If you behave sensibly here, I will put no obstacles in the way of your marriage."

"What, in the name of all the Western Isles, has today's meeting to do with my marriage?"

28

There was a wistfulness in his manner as he resumed. "I must not keep it a secret from you, Klantor—I am far from well. My damaged heart will never be sound again. In the small time left to me, I want to see Lampra provided for. Ever since her mother's death fifteen summers ago, she has been all to me. I have brought her up as well as I could, with the help of Testa, who has been servant, nurse, and foster mother. For her sake, I was happy at your betrothal."

"Then, Argillon," I interrupted, "why have you changed? I still love her more than my own heart's blood."

"Now you grow sentimental," he broke in, with a disapproving gesture. "The fact is this, my young friend, you have taken a step that would subject her, as your wife, to injury, insult, and neglect. That is why I have forbidden her to see you. But if at the next meeting of the *Kolem* you should reform your ways, then I can see no reason why your marriage should not take place as originally intended."

I gasped; I stammered; at first I was incapable of coherent speech. Angrily I ranged the room.

"So, Argillon!" I demanded. "Either I betray my love, or I betray all the people of the Western Isles!"

"I would not put it like that," he denied, with a suave half-smile. "Say, rather, that you will either be reasonable or dash your head against the rocks. If after three more sunrises, at the next meeting of the *Kolem*, you act with the intelligence that I know you possess, then all that has happened will be a forgotten wisp of fog!"

He adjusted his *changus*; picked up a little book; and hardly cast me a glance as I went slumping out.

Back and forth and around and around I paced in my circular room on the top floor of the *Kra-tho* or

Municipal Bachelor Dormitories. A fair green island kept coming before me, gay with a brilliance of flowers and an exuberance of bird song; and suddenly it would disappear in a flare of smoke and steam, while the skies turned red and black, and men and women gasped out their lives in a sulphurous gale, and the sea rolled in and covered all.

And then I knew that I could not betray my responsibility. No, I must fight on against the destruction of the Cocoanut Islands. If I gave up for the sake of my love for Lampra, would I not prove myself unworthy of that love? Actually, there was no choice.

Nevertheless, the decision was made not by my reason but by some power deeper than reason. Though the world might condemn me, though I might be taking a fool's dive to disaster, I could act in only one way.

Long before the cheery light of dawn had crept over the city, I had planned my course. My first move would be to organize all the support I could from such of the *Kolem* as were halfway on my side. As soon as the hour permitted, therefore, I visited the home of old Velto Vanrr, the representative of the *Clotilla* or scholars.

As I drew near his house, I was sure that I saw Vanrr's white-haired figure through the crystalline panels of the sun room at one end of the building. But a servant returned with the halting statement that, "Professor Vanrr—he has just left, and will not be back for two days."

I had no better success when I went to see Tellin Trus, the delegate of the *Vrontal*, or artists and literary men; his wife made a hasty excuse. "Too bad, Councillor, he is sick in bed."

Tired and discouraged, I sought Dr. Zuno Klan, the representative of the biologists and physicians. But at Klan's office, an assistant nervously informed me,

30

"You've picked the wrong day, sir. Dr. Klan can find time to see nobody today. . . . No, not tomorrow, either."

Three tries—three failures! Was this just a triple coincidence?

Now for the next part of my plan. After dragging my way back to my room, where I snatched a few hours' disturbed sleep, I returned to Argillon's estate and began watching some of the walks leading out. If I could only catch sight of Lampra, I would bear her off with me!

Unfortunately, the walks were empty. And so after a time, having devised a scheme, I made my way to the rear of the spacious grounds, and sought the gardener Ru Manir, whom I found trimming a hedge.

"Maybe, Ru," I suggested, "as you love your mistress, you will take another message for me?"

Ru went on clipping the briars. .

"I dislike to disappoint you, Councillor," he answered, after a minute. "But by Ablum! that poor young thing is followed around so closely by the old watch-owl that I can't be sure who would get the message. If I were caught—well, after all, Councillor, I'm an old man."

I thanked Ru and went my way. His refusal had been the last of a series of sledgehammer blows.

CHAPTER V

ALONE AGAINST THE PACK

After several evenings' leave of absence, I returned that night to Mt. Nublis Observatory, where I was employed as a *cullum* or assistant Star Watcher.

As I adjusted the camera to the great new reflecting telescope, I spoke with the *Arcullum* or Head Star Watcher, Langhis Ghand. He was a man of forty-five summers, with hair once brick-red, now streaked with iron-gray; wide, clear, open face; and shining, large, candid gray eyes. Despite our difference in age, we were fast friends.

Taking advantage of the absence of my assistant, Yonner Du, Langhis came to me and put a brotherly arm about my shoulders.

"Klantor, old comrade! You look like a whipped dog."

I turned to him sadly. "No use trying to hide the truth from you, Langhis! At the meeting of the *Kolem,* I found myself crossing daggers with almost everyone, especially Wauglan Waud."

Langhis took a stride or two about the large, glass-enclosed room.

"Let me counsel you, Klantor. Waud is the most ruthless man in the Western Isles. Remember Vice-Marshal Murtal, who had the folly to oppose him, and was found mysteriously dead?"

"Yes, yes, I know," I interrupted, for the episode was familiar to everyone. "As I love our Xandu, I wouldn't oppose him if it were not a matter of principle."

"Principle or no principle, Waud will strike you down like a mosquito!" Langhis insisted. "By great Ablum, Klantor! we need you here in the observatory."

I turned away without a word. But he was still eyeing me intently as I made some pretended adjustment in the camera.

"There's some deeper reason," he said, "or I'm no interpreter of stars or hearts."

With a groan, I sank down upon a bench.

"There *is* some deeper reason, Langhis. Because of my dispute with Waud, Argillon forbids me to see his daughter."

My friend threw his head back in a short, not unsympathetic laugh.

"Oh, is that all? Such little love difficulties—well, you know, Klantor, I've had them myself. What worries me is Wauglan Waud," Langhis plunged back to the attack. "I urge you, Klantor—don't stand in his path!"

Langhis' warning was to come back to me two or

33

three days later, when I attended the next meeting of the *Kolem*.

I had taken care not to be ahead of time, and several of my colleagues had preceded me to the Golden Conclave Hall, where they all stood together in one corner, chatting beneath the bronze busts of the old leaders of the Western Isles. Not one of them seemed aware of my presence.

Unhappily, I took a seat. After a little while, Argillon came in, gave me a chilly nod, and stared at me with a faint quizzical smile. I could almost read his thought: "Well, my boy, are you going to be sensible? But of course, no man in his right mind would turn from a bright career, an advantageous marriage, praise and fame."

This imagined mindreading only made me clench my fists more firmly and once more swear to myself not to surrender. But would I have the strength?

As the meeting began, Drandro-dra's eyes had a glitter as of sunlight on lead. In words that echoed those of the previous session, he intoned the opening prayer; in a mealy voice, he placed before us various matters on which we cast a routine vote. Finally, with a slanted grin, he turned to Wauglan Waud, who had sat throughout the proceedings with the face of a carved god.

"Now, honored Lord Defender," he announced, "we return to the matter you discussed at our last meeting. Have you anything more to say?"

Waud arose like a gigantic cork popped out of a bottle. The platinum decorations clattered on his broad chest; his square jaw, beneath the bull-like gray head, shot forward.

"My brothers of the *Kolem*," he began, in that squeaking feminine voice, "it is time to vote on the new defenses. The problem is even more urgent than I had supposed. Here—" He paused, and pulled a

34

sheaf of blue papers from an inner pocket. "Here is momentous new evidence, just placed before me by the Secret Eyes."

Waud let a weighted moment pass.

"I have here some data of so select a nature," he went on, "that I cannot divulge it, my brothers. I can, however, reveal its general nature, which is that the Eastern Islanders, with diabolical craftiness, have been perfecting dreadful new weapons to turn against us when we are least prepared. No answer is possible except new and even more potent defenses—all of which, as you see, proves all the more how right I was at our last meeting."

To my own surprise, I was on my feet. "Distinguished Wauglan Waud, maybe you will give us some idea of these new weapons of the Eastern Islanders?"

"Impossible!" he snapped. "The Armed Defenders have marked them 'Supreme Secrecy.' For the sake of our national safety, you must take my word."

"But honorable Wauglan Waud, it is the business of the *Kolem* to use its own intelligence. We are not children—we must have the facts before we can judge."

"*I* have the facts!" stormed Waud. "That should be enough—that is, if you really have your country's good at heart!"

He halted just long enough for the imputations to sink in, then began pounding the table until it rattled.

"But come! We waste words! Let us get to the vote! Let me say this," Waud went on. "At the last meeting, we heard some immoderate opinions. But I feel sure of greater sanity today. If everyone votes as our national good demands, then I for one, being of a forgiving nature, will overlook all that has been said as the mere rashness of youth. But do not forget this, my brothers—the law requires a *unanimous* vote!"

As Waud popped back into his seat, the soft-tongued Drandro-dra once more spoke.

"Remember, brothers, the vote today will be to authorize an experiment leading to artificial volcanic eruptions, by which we hope to eliminate the Cocoanut Island of Zuttel. I myself, as the head of the *Kolem*, vote for the experiment. Now, Argillon, as second on the voting list, what do you say?"

Argillon smiled in a chilly way and voted with Drandro-dra. And so did Wauglan Waud, Yunto Ghratt, Zuno Klan, and another member. At length it was the turn of white-haired Velto Vanrr, the appointee of the *Clotilla* or scholars, one of the two who had sided with me.

Velto hesitated. A long, leaden moment went by. His head dropped; in a low voice, which I could barely make out, he said, "I—I, my brothers, vote for the experiment."

Clearly as in a flashlight picture, everything stood revealed; I knew how Waud had cajoled, threatened, browbeaten poor old Velto during the days since the last meeting.

Then, too, I knew how my remaining supporter, Tellin Trus, would cast his vote.

Never had I felt more alone than after hearing Drandro-dra's triumphant pronouncement, "Eight votes! Eight in favor of the experiment! Now, except for our latest and youngest member, it is unanimous. So what does he say?"

As I arose, I saw all eyes—hard eyes, unfriendly eyes—staring at me in silent inquiry. And I knew, with a terrible clarity, that my words would determine my fate.

"Well, what does our latest and youngest member say?"

"I—I, my brothers, I vote against the experiment."

As I sank back into my seat, I could see the fiery

flashes in the eyes of my colleagues—could see Argillon's surprised glitter, and the bovine glare of Wauglan Waud as he once more shot out of his seat.

"The young member should remember," he squeaked at me, "that one man cannot set himself against a nation! One man cannot block the defenses of the Western Isles!"

His thick, blunt forefinger pointed at me with reproach.

"I predict this!" he shrilled, stamping with one foot. "The oversure fledgling will yet change his vote—that is, if he wishes to enjoy life in the Western Isles!"

Little wonder that, as Drandro-dra intoned the closing prayer and my fellow members began filing out without a glance in my direction, I felt more alone than ever.

Again, above the scraping of feet and the mumblings of my colleagues, I seemed to hear the Seeress of the Dawn, "Small storms precede great! Small storms precede great! Small storms precede great!"

CHAPTER VI

SHADOWS AND SWORD THRUSTS

Day after day I had haunted the vicinity of Argillon's home, on the off chance that I might see Lampra. It would be useless to seek to reach her in any less direct way, since a letter was sure to be intercepted. But apparently all my restless rovings could gain me nothing. Of Lampra I saw no sign.

I did, however, make a disturbing discovery. From time to time, I saw a thin little man in a dark tunic weaving his way behind me. Hoping to shake him off, I would wind afoot through long devious streets; but always, like a dogged rear guard, he would reappear. Several times I approached him to demand what he wanted, but always he vanished like a rat into a hole. Meanwhile, despising myself for the precaution, I purchased an *assugut*, a small razor-bladed dagger,

38

which I concealed in its sheath beneath my tunic.

Six or eight days after my second experience with the *Kolem*, I received a new shock. One morning I chanced to pass through the *Romul* or central square of the city, an open space where many-colored fountains splashed and date-palms rose high above banks of hibiscus and oleander. At one corner, a crowd stood before a tall yellowish-white wall, on which large moving letters were flashed from a distant reflector—the latest reports of the *Drust*, the Central Information Service. As was my habit, I joined the many who stood open-mouthed while bulletin followed bulletin.

The spectators made way for me respectfully, bowing with murmurs of recognition—thanks to the fact that my picture, when I joined the *Kolem*, had been flashed on the *Klar* or viewing screen.

Then I let my eyes follow the announcements on the wall, and after a time I was stunned by a name.

"Argillon," I read, "the distinguished member of the *Kolem*, and eminent *Hassessi*, left today in his private pleasure ship *Coral Reef* on a voyage of indefinite duration to foreign ports, as an envoy of good will for the Western Isles. The companion of his travels is his young daughter . . ."

Clapping one hand over my forehead, which had begun to ache, I staggered away. I was unaware of the crowd; all that I knew was that Lampra, *my* Lampra, was now far away, on an adventure that might take her from me forever. Oh, why, why had she sent me no message?

Blindly, I made my way out of the *Romul* into an unfrequented side street, wandering at random. As I glanced back from an intersection, I chanced to see a figure some distance behind, recognized the thin little man in the dark tunic, who had been following me for days, and could not keep back the obvious conclusion.

The man had not, after all, been put on my trail by Argillon. And if not by Argillon, then by whom? A chill went down my spine at the obvious answer.

Hours later, returning to my dormitory room, I was about to throw myself half exhausted onto the cot, when my eyes fell upon a little green-sealed document on the table. The heavy printed lettering was that of the *Panju*, public message carriers, and what a start I gave when my eyes fell upon the contents!— the small, shapely handwriting, and the familiar private symbol, "X * * X":

> *Dearest and most precious,*
> *I am able to get this to the* Panju *only in a stolen moment, when Testa is too busy packing to notice. I must be brief, for fear of being found out. Father is forcing me to leave with him on a very long cruise, maybe for a whole year or more. Testa is to come too. I have wept so much! But be of good cheer, beloved. You have my heart forever. Surely the gods will bring us together again sometime. Now I must close. I hear Testa shuffling about in the next room. I will give this letter to Ru Manir, who will deliver it to the* Panju. *And now goodbye—until we next meet.*
>
> *Your Ever-Devoted Lampra*

Reverently, I fondled the paper and stood clutching it like a sacred relic, while I stared with moist eyes at the city's twinkling night expanses, wondering why I had let love slip from my hands.

In my despair, as I ranged about the circular dormitory room, I thought of taking my own life. There were drugs that would accomplish this swiftly and dependably. But the idea was no sooner born than it died within me. What! take the coward's road? Would that not merely deliver an easy victory to my ene-

40

mies? If I did not remain in the *Kolem* to vote against volcanic warfare, my successor certainly would vote for it.

Besides, was Lampra really gone from me forever? I could not share her own lovable, simple faith that the gods would surely bring us together sometime. Yet I knew that however long her voyage, it could not continue indefinitely. A year, perhaps even two years —and she would be back. And who knew but that her father could then be circumvented?

Meanwhile my salvation would be to engulf myself in my work. Through my interest in the outer galaxies, I would lose some of the heartache of my recent human contacts.

How little I realized that my troubles were only beginning!

A few days after receiving Lampra's letter, I chanced to pass again through the central square or *Romul*, and paused once more before the *Klar* or viewing screen. But now, to my surprise, the people did not make way for me with respectful bows. In several throats there were low mutterings of revulsion. Women drew up their tunics, as if from contact with a snake or toad; urchins jeered, and one struck me with a pellet of mud; I heard my name spoken with a hiss by one of the men. What had I done to make myself so unpopular?

I was still pondering this question that evening when I reached the Observatory. As I entered, I was greeted by sub-Assistant Yonner Du, whose lean, wry face was twisted into a smirk.

"Ah, here comes the great man!" he threw out, as he turned from the eyepiece of the huge reflector. "Maybe you'll tell me, good Councillor, what is this I'm hearing about you?"

"How can I tell you what you're hearing?" I snapped, not liking his insinuating tone.

41

"I'm only hearing what's common gossip all over town, old fellow. I assure you, I don't believe a word of it—not a single dirty word!"

"Dirty word of what?" I demanded.

Yonner's smirk grew still broader; his gray-green eyes sparkled with malicious amusement.

"Really, old fellow, I hate to repeat such a bundle of lies. Why, the story goes that while you revel in luxury, you neglect your old mother, who lives in rags in the *Hrotiut*—"

"How could I neglect my mother," I roared, "when she died the day I was born?"

"Which only proves, old fellow," acknowledged Yonner, suavely, "it's all nothing but a bag of lies. The same with the story about Argillon's daughter."

I jumped as if a hammer had pounded my sore thumb. "What about Argillon's daughter?" I yelled.

He slank back, but the glitter of evil relish had not left his eyes.

"It's not really what they say about her, old fellow —it's what they say about you. That the lady dismissed you after finding you'd been keeping house with one of the *heptan*, having a son by one."

Blankly I stared at my colleague. The *heptan* were the lowest offshoots of the female population of the Western Isles.

"Why, in the name of great Ablum," I shouted, with the outraged consciousness of innocence, "I never, never once—"

"Don't I know it?" acknowledged Yonner, still with the same smirk. "You're a good, honorable fellow, pure as the white camellia. I'm enraged at your being slandered by all those other stories—"

Before he could say what the other stories were, the door opened, and Head Star Watcher Langhis Ghand stepped in.

Apparently he had heard Yonner's last words; for

42

he stood staring at his sub-assistant, then growled, "Get back to your work, Yonner! Don't you ever again torment Klantor with those ridiculous yarns!"

"So you've heard them, too?" I asked, after Langhis had led me aside to the computation room.

"Yes—who hasn't? It's only what I feared, Klantor —and the least of what I've feared. You'll have to be resigned to persecution if you stand in the way of a man like Wauglan Waud."

"So you think Waud's responsible?"

"How can I doubt it? You'll be lucky if he stops at this point."

"Apparently he hasn't stopped there," I confided. And I told how I had been followed—was still being followed—by the mysterious small man in the dark tunic.

"There's nothing you can do, Klantor, but try to outlive it and overcome Waud's enmity, if you can," advised Langhis, putting an affectionate arm about my shoulder.

But I was not consoled. I felt I was grappling with some formless monster which was wrapping its coils about me more and more.

CHAPTER VII

TWO BLACK MESSAGES

Back from the Observatory after my talk with Langhis, I found a message awaiting me in my room, headed by the official crimson inscription of the *Kra-tho* or Municipal Bachelor Dormitories.

Honored Klantor Fey,
    This is to notify you that, ten noons hence, at the end of your present rental period, we will require your room and hence request you to find new quarters.

                    Gro Dunthryu,
                    Manager the Kra-tho

My first impulse was to rush down to see Gro Dunthryu, but I realized that this would accomplish nothing; he was a mere pawn in other hands. This was the only time, to my knowledge, that anyone had ever been asked to leave the *Kra-tho*, except for some good reason.

But I was not being expelled as a bad tenant. I was being persecuted—the butt of a monstrous enmity.

I was all the unhappier since my room, with its sweeping view, was an especially favored one; besides, I had grown used to the only home I had known for years. But no doubt I would find something else that pleased me well enough.

When I began looking, however, I received some further shocks. There were, truly, many suitable unoccupied rooms and suites of rooms—but why was it that some obstacle always arose? Perhaps the owner would recognize me, and haltingly mutter an excuse. Or else the arrangements would be all but made, and then, after asking my name, the prospective renter would grow embarrassed, would gasp, stammer, and blurt out that he had forgotten a promise to another applicant. After a dozen rebuffs, I realized the depth to which the slanders against me had penetrated.

Finally, I turned in desperation to one of the *Krous* or "anthill districts," the *Hrotiut*, the home not only of the very poor, but of thieves, vagabonds, and ruffians. Here no questions would be asked. But here vile odors of refuse and sewage filled the stagnant air between the immense stone buildings. The streets were of a pattern found nowhere else in the city; in the center a dark pavement was filled with rattling hand-drawn carts and gliding *littos*; beyond iron railings, on each side of the pavement, a dim, narrow ravine reached down further than a man could jump. And these ravines, threaded by footpaths where pedestrians swarmed, too often could be reached only by long wire ladders.

"It will be only for a day or two, until I find something better," I reassured myself, as I moved into a

45

tiny back room, which looked out upon a stone court so enclosed by tall brick and stone that it was twilight even at noon.

Had any Councillor of the Western Isles, I wondered, ever before been reduced to such an extremity?

Meanwhile I continued to attend the secret meetings of the *Kolem*. And every session was like an icebath; no one ever spoke to me. But at every meeting, one important matter came up: Wauglan Waud invariably moved for a fresh vote on his proposed volcanic experiment, and invariably mine was the solitary dissenting voice. The strategy, apparently, was to wear me out.

Meanwhile, like the manipulators of a torture machine, my adversaries were piling even greater weights upon me. Their next blow, launched from an unexpected quarter, did indeed make me cry out.

One evening, on reaching the Observatory for my night's work, I was coughing a bit, and was feeling sadder than ever at the thought of Lampra, from whom I had had no word in the many days since her departure. What was happening to her?

I had hardly entered when I noticed the look on the face of my friend, Langhis Ghand. His whole appearance reflected pain, which had put furrows on his sage, broad forehead, and made his long, sensitive hands flutter nervously.

For a moment he stared at me sorrowfully. When he spoke, his low, vibrant voice reinforced the impression of pain. "Klantor, my friend! I've been waiting to talk to you."

Ony then did I notice the long, purple-sealed document which he picked up from a small stand at his side.

At the top, printed in bright gold, I saw the figures of two eagles perched side by side on a rocky eyrie.

46

"The *Thadros!*" I exclaimed, recognizing the insignia of the triumvirate, the theoretical rulers of the Western Isles, most of whose powers had been taken over by the *Kolem.* "But what, in high Ablum's name—"

"You may well wonder, my friend. You realize, of course, they still retain some powers."

"Yes, such as to act as a court in cases of treason. But what has that to do with you?"

"They also have the right to make and withdraw appointments," Langhis said pointedly. "But here! read this, Klantor!"

With a hasty thrust, he passed me the gold-printed document. The letters did a devils' dance before my eyes as I glanced beyond the polite formalities to the harsh meaning:

Estimable Langhis Ghand
Head Star Watcher
Mt. Nublis Observatory
    We present our compliments, Honored Sir.
    By virtue of our high office, we have the privilege of informing you that we have appointed the eminent scientist Qucn Poiuyu to be Assistant Star Watcher at your Observatory. Upon his arrival, three nights hence, he is to relieve the present Assistant of his duties.
    Your servants in all things,

                    Poco Xantyl
                 Amano Thythib
                 Khrillut Tho
       Thadros of the Western Isles

A minute had passed before I could blurt out a half coherent reply.

"This—this—by all the gods, Langhis, I've never heard of anything to match it!"

"Nor have I," concurred Langhis, absently picking up the letter. "I've never known the *Thadros* to interfere before in scientific appointments."

"Who's this 'eminent Quon Poiuyu'?" I demanded. "Ever heard of him, Langhis?"

Langhis shook his head sadly.

"Well, by Ablum," I stormed, "he's nothing but a political tool. But to be thrown out for some unknown hack—"

I sputtered; I choked on my own words.

Langhis came to my side, and I felt a brotherly arm about my shoulders.

"Listen, Klantor old friend! If anyone deserves this job, you do. You've worked for it; you're fitted for it. And in the interests of science, *I* want you here!"

I had slumped down upon a bench, and he seated himself next to me.

"But if I protested, the gods would laugh," he meditated.

"I never thought Wauglan would strike a foul blow like this," I mourned. "That is, if it was *he!*"

"Who else could it be?"

I was silent. If Waud had been able to unseat me from Mt. Nublis Observatory, then there was not another position of the kind open to me in all the Western Isles, since all astronomers were Government employees.

"Why, it's nothing but tyranny!" I growled.

"All government, Klantor, tends toward tyranny. I don't have to tell you, I'm as badly shattered by this as you. But I too am only an employee. Now I'm worried for your sake. If you're ever in trouble—if you need help, or merely want friendly advice and consultation—always remember this! Mine is one door you must never be afraid to knock at!"

Both his hands reached out and held mine in a long, steady grip.

48

CHAPTER VIII

THE PROPOSAL OF XARDIS BLAN

"No, no, honored sir, no opening today. Try down the street. The gods be with you, honored sir!"

· Not once, but a hundred times, I had met the same rebuff. For many days I had been seeking any work I felt at all qualified for; but it was just as when I had looked for living quarters: as soon as I was recognized, or as soon as my name was mentioned, the prospective employer would freeze.

Bitterly I reflected on an old saying, that when the gods decide to strip a man, they strip him clean. Well, at least, there was now little more for the gods to take from me.

After a time, I realized that if I did not wish to starve (since my work for the *Kolem* was honorary, and unpaid), there were two things I must do: take

49

an assumed name, and wear a disguise. Hence I began introducing myself by the name of my mother's father, Munjin Alg. And I began growing a beard, and hid my eyes beneath wide, deeply tinted blue-green glasses. But as an unknown and unrecommended applicant, I could expect only the most menial job.

Even menial jobs, however, were not easy to get. Daily I would go to the *Romul* and stand amid a tattered crowd when the list of job offerings was flashed on the bulletin wall. But little good any of these seemed to do me. A would-be employer would glance at my hands and decide that I was not fitted to be a coal heaver or a hauler of freight. Days went by; my small reserves were being exhausted. I ate as meagerly as possible, yet had to sell all my clothes except the ones I wore, and was at the point of selling my *litto*, without which I could not get about the city.

Then one morning I saw a notation from the *Panju* or public message service:

WANTED: Message carrier. Must have litto, *and must know the city. Experience not necessary. Apply, Zuggut Butru, Manager.*

I made my way without eagerness to the office of Zuggut Butru, for message-carrying was held to be one of the lowest of occupations. Still, I was hungry —very hungry.

Zuggut Butru was a fat-faced man who sat amid piles of pillows on an office divan. He did not ask me to be seated, but immediately growled, "Have you a *litto?*"

"Yes, thanks to the gods."

"Are you ready to start at once?"

"At once."

"What did you say your name is?"

50

"Munjin Alg."

"Munjin Alg?" he repeated, suspiciously. "Very well. Your wage will be half an *Atlantid* a day. Take this blue slip to the clerk in the office to your right."

By this time, my beard had grown considerably. Even so, I was afraid that some old friend would recognize me as I went whisking to all parts of the city. And though I now had work, I could not live on my wages—I needed also the small gratuities, *baggleto*, which I never took without wincing; especially as I was expected to address the donors with head bent low.

Was there no escape for me? Since I could find no other employment, it almost seemed so. Ah, if I could have seen where my path was leading when I had so boldly opposed Wauglan Waud, would I have had the courage to strike?

So I asked myself, as I went flitting about on my *litto*. Then suddenly an unlooked-for deliverance opened before me.

One morning, just as I left the *Hall of the Kolem*—for I still attended each session of the legislators, doggedly blocking Waud's proposal—I was accosted by a dapper little man in a red-and-green plaid tunic.

"Councillor Klantor Fey! May I beg a word?"

"What do you want?" I demanded, noting his fox-like features.

"Something that, by great Ablum! it will benefit you to hear. Perhaps you will do me the honor to accompany me to my home, just beyond the next turn?"

"I never enter unknown homes!"

The stranger laughed. "I admire your caution, Councillor," he said, "But I am really your friend. What if we go beneath the trees of the *Kolem* park?"

I nodded. In the public park, facing the *Hall of the Kolem*, I would be safe.

51

"My name is Xardis Blan," he introduced himself. "For days I have been seeking you. By the nine gods of Mt. Nublis and their nine goddesses! you were hard to recognize in that black beard. And hard to find!"

This, truly, was the case. Recently I had left my room in the *Hrotiut* district for less repulsive quarters; to avoid possible enemies, I had given no forwarding address. If I had not attended the meetings of the *Kolem*, there would have been no clue to my whereabouts.

Without a word, I followed my new acquaintance to a spot beneath the trees of the *Kolem* park, within sight of passersby, yet sufficiently secluded not to be overheard. With a wry grimace, Xardis Blan smoothed out his tunic and seated himself beside me. For half a minute he sat staring at me with a quizzical smile on his tricky-looking face; then he spoke in tones as smooth as oil.

"Klantor Fey! I come as the emissary of one who bears you nothing but good will—one who wishes to extricate you from your net of difficulties."

"Yes? Who is this benevolent friend?"

"That, Councillor Fey, I am not permitted to state. But I assume that the name of your rescuer will matter little so long as he restores you to the sunlight."

"You speak in enigmas," I said.

His quick eyes glanced warily to all sides. And then, having made sure that no one was within hearing distance, he resumed in low tones:

"Would you like, Councillor Fey, to climb back to where you were before you became a Councillor?"

"Would I not like," I gibed, "to return to the sweet days of last summer?"

Xardis' voice, as he continued, had a syrupy quality. "You are a skeptical man, Councillor Fey; I commend your circumspection. It happens, however, that I have nothing impossible in mind. Let us begin with one small matter. Formerly, you occupied quarters in the *Kra-tho?*"

I nodded.

"To your backer, it would take but the flick of a finger to induce the manager to restore your old apartment, or another equally good. Would that not interest you?"

I shifted uneasily, and absently tossed several pebbles at a log.

"No, Xardis Blan, that would not interest me. I no longer have the means for the dormitory room."

"But by Ablum! what if we enabled you to meet the rent?"

"*We?* Who do you mean by *we?*" I asked, sharply.

"Only the backer I mentioned before, Councillor. By speaking to the *Thadros* and convincing them that they acted too hastily, perhaps he can restore your post at Mt. Nublis."

A silence followed.

"Why would this man—this mysterious backer—want to restore my post at the Observatory?"

"For your sake—and the country's," answered Xardis, in tones that did not convince me.

"Maybe he'll also restore my lost reputation?"

"Well, why not?" My interviewer's eyes glittered like a raven's. "After all, what can be done can be undone. If any stories did you an injustice, Councillor, new reports can be spread through the same channels. Is it not true, by the way, that you were betrothed to one of Kallendra's choicest daughters?"

As if someone had rapped me in the face, I shot forward.

"In delicate matters like these, your backer prefers not to intrude," the speaker went on suavely, "but it

53

may interest you to know that he is not without influence with the lady's father."

A vision of Lampra's animated features flashed over me: her dark eyes dancing beneath tall bunched coppery hair. "By great Ablum! would I not give my right arm—"

I stopped short, seeing the glitter in the stranger's foxlike eyes.

"Then it might all be arranged, Councillor—when Argillon returns with his daughter from their voyage. Indeed, he might be induced to cut the voyage short."

Ah, why was my interviewer tormenting me?

"I see you're still not convinced," Xardis went on. "Then you do not believe that anyone in all the Western Isles is powerful enough to do all I have suggested?"

"I would be a fool to believe!"

Xardis smiled with an icy amusement.

"Councillor, I see that we understand one another. You are a man of the world—you know that everything today has its price. But the payment will be no more than you can afford."

Some children, dashing past us with shouts and yells, created a momentary interruption. Then, with a slow incisiveness, the stranger went on.

"I understand that at a meeting of the *Kolem*, Councillor, you opposed the other members on an important issue."

I jerked myself up abruptly; rose to my full height. "That may or may not be true. What of it?"

"Well, Councillor, your backer is interested above all things in the good of the Western Isles. He holds that disharmony in the *Kolem* is not in the best interests of the Isles. Therefore, if this cleavage can be ended—"

I stood glowering at the stranger. "What's that?" I demanded. "You're suggesting I barter my vote?"

54

"Sit down, Councillor, please!" begged Xardis. "Not so loud, in the gods' names. You leap to conclusions," he went on, in muffled tones. "Your backer does not ask you to change your vote."

"No? What then?"

Xardis' tones became softer, wheedling.

"He understands that for a man of honor a turnabout in voting would be impossible. The loss of face—"

"It's not only the loss of face!"

"Certainly not. Your backer suggests a way of saving your face, and your honor, too."

"And what's this miraculous remedy?"

"It's not miraculous. Merely sensible. You'll resign as one of the *Kolem*—"

I sputtered, growled in anger. Nevertheless, a tempting thought did come to me—might this not be the way out?

"I have no reason to resign."

"Your health, Councillor."

"My health, thanks be to the gods, is excellent."

"Ill health, as you know, is an excuse ready-made by the gods. Besides," Xardis hastened on blandly, "I can give you assurances that my promises are more than wind."

"First," I pleaded, anxious to end the interview, "I need time—time to think."

Xardis grinned.

"Here, take this," he said, reaching into his tunic for a small stamped metallic plaque, which I took without a word. "You can find me at this address. I'll expect to hear from you, Councillor, within three days."

As he arose, he continued, with just the hint of a hiss, "I must add this, Councillor. Your backer, being a humane man, prefers gentle ways. But if you foolishly refuse his generosity, a time may come when

55

you'll act under unhappier circumstances. Remember
—I'll be awaiting word."

He waved; smiled with a saturnine twist of his lean
features; and started off along a winding clay path.

CHAPTER IX

A DECISION AND A WARNING

As I skimmed along the streets to deliver my messages for the *Panju*, my mind was on one message only: the one from my mysterious interviewer. I was really tempted, for I did not doubt that my enemies could restore most of what they had taken from me. Why should they not, if incidentally they got what they wanted?

Still in a turmoil, I halted my *litto* in a parking strip of the *Cordocco*, where I found a bench, and for some time sat looking out at the *littos* flitting along the wide granite-paved esplanade.

Clearly, I was at a turning point from which I might go on either to darkness or joy. But when had life ever brought much joy to me? I recalled my stern, loveless childhood as the ward of a fault-finding old

57

aunt. I remembered how, to escape from the world's harshness, I had taken to studying the stars; had been granted a *vral* or scholarship, and had gradually made my way in my profession, though little light or gladness had come to me until my meeting with Lampra at a reception given by the *Nuftt* or Guild of Scientists.

I went on in a colloquy with myself: "Are you running away like a frightened child? Is it any less dishonorable to resign from the *Kolem* than to vote with your opponents?"

Into my mind, at the same time, the vision returned of a fair island, with green hill-forests, sky-blue lakes, and flowering fields; and all at once I saw it wreathed in licking fires and dirty-yellow sulphurous fumes. And I knew that this would be but the beginning should volcanic warfare be tolerated.

No, no, though the whole world stood against me, I must not compromise, I must not surrender. My happiness, or the happiness of a hundred, a thousand like me—what was this compared with the very life of Atlantis?

As I arose from the bench, I raised two imploring hands to heaven. And then, reaching into the folds of my tunic, I seized the little stamped metallic plaque containing the address of Xardis Blan, and flung it far into the shrubbery.

Fifteen days went by, while I lived like one who dreads to see unknown swordsmen behind every post and wall. I went nowhere without concealing my *assugut* securely inside my tunic.

But I had not foreseen the direction of the attack.

Returning one day to my room, I found a message beneath the door, which was surprising, for only one person knew where I was.

But the paper was indeed from the one person to whom I had given my address:

Klantor, My Friend:
  Come at once. It is urgent.

Langhis Ghand.

What could this mean? Never before had the Head Star Watcher visited my humble quarters; only an extraordinary need could have brought him to this mean district.

An hour later, my *litto* had carried me to his home, which overlooked the city from the lower slopes of Mt. Nublis. Great sunset clouds had gathered serenely above the broad, smoldering bay, but there was no serenity in my heart, nor in my friend's.

"Ah, Klantor, I was awaiting you," he threw out, as he led me in. It seemed to me that he had aged in the few weeks since we had met, his red hair now more gray-streaked. "Be seated on those cushions, Klantor. Surely, you're hungry after your trip here. Let's have a little *mevot.*"

Having served this food, Langhis cleared his throat, bent forward on his pile of cushions, and pointed a long, lean finger at me as if in warning.

"Maybe, Klantor, my message alarmed you?"

"Maybe."

"You were right to be apprehensive. You haven't been in touch, of course, with recent doings at the *Nuftt?*" he went on, with seeming irrelevance, referring to the nation-wide guild of scientists which had appointed me as its representative to the *Kolem.*

"Unfortunately, I've been out of touch with the world. But what has the *Nuftt* to do with my being here today?"

He paused, and chewed uneasily at his thin, clean-

59

shaven underlip. "I'll not conceal the facts, Klantor. Termites have been burrowing in the dark."

"Termites?" I demanded, springing to my feet.

"Please sit down. Hear me out. It makes me writhe to mention this, Klantor, but here is the simple truth. The *Nuftt* is entitled, as you know, to withdraw your appointment at any time."

I groaned. "So someone is maneuvering to recall me from the *Kolem?*"

"Someone? No, an organized group. The matter comes up tomorrow. I've just had it from Yonner Du. He got it, I gather, from some connection of his on the Committee."

"By great Ablum!" I exclaimed, rising again and pounding the air. "I knew those fiends were out for my blood!"

"Well, it *is* unusual," Langhis conceded. "Besides, it was accomplished with such spiderlike secrecy you and I mightn't have had any chance to answer the charges—"

"Charges? What charges? How can they bring charges against me?"

"Be calm, Klantor! The charges—I'm not sure of the details. According to Yonner, they're based on the general idea that you haven't served the interests of us scientists at meetings of the *Kolem.*"

"But who knows what's done by the *Kolem?*" I stormed.

Langhis sat gravely stroking his chin. "You imagine, I'm sure, that you've preserved secrecy about a certain invention that was mentioned to the *Kolem*. Am I wrong in saying it had to do with a new weapon—the weapon of man-made volcanic eruptions?"

I stared. I gasped. My head whirled. "How—how under the stars, Langhis—"

With a joyless triumph, he smiled at my confusion. "You're a scientist yourself, Klantor. You know that

60

the weapon was not devised by any of the *Kolem*. Down to the last detail, it was conceived and planned by scientists. Many of them share the supposed secret. And scientists are but human. The knowledge has seeped out, though as yet only to other scientists. It's known that you, Klantor, you alone, have blocked the new weapon. Hence the accusation that, in obstructing scientific advance, you have been unfaithful to the men who elected you to the *Kolem*."

A moment passed. Never had I heard anything more unjust.

"I don't blame you for your position, Klantor," Langhis droned on. "But one man cannot block the rush of destiny. Your only chance will be to defend yourself at the meeting tomorrow."

"But how can I, when the matters can't be discussed? To tell what went on at the meeting of the *Kolem* would be to violate my oath."

"You needn't violate any oath, Klantor. You need only talk in generalities. Everyone—never fear!—will know what you mean."

I started up and warmly seized both his hands.

Disapprovingly he eyed my frayed, dark, dust-stained tunic. "Listen, Klantor, you'll have a better chance before the *Nuftt* in other clothes, which I can lend you. Also, if you remove that ragged black brush from your face—"

"No, that's impossible!" I argued, and explained once more my need of retaining my disguise.

"Be here tomorrow at the seventh hour, and we'll go together to the meeting," he went on, glancing out of the window toward a sky from which the last glint of daylight had vanished. "Well, I must be off to the Observatory."

Perhaps he noticed how I winced, for he went on, "There's never a night, Klantor, but that I miss you up

61

at Mt. Nublis. Ah, well, you'll get back there someday!"

But I knew that he had no faith in such a possibility. And when we parted company, a chill shot down
my spine though the evening was not cold.

"Small storms precede great! Small storms precede
great!" the warning of the Seeress of the Dawn kept
echoing through my mind. "Small storms—small
storms precede great!"

CHAPTER X

THE BATTLE OF THE NUFTT

The meeting place of the Managing Committee of the *Nuftt* was a wide, open court between two great buildings, where it was seated in an elevated semicircular cushioned bench. Rows of cushions, in nine concentric circles along the ground, provided seats for as many members of the *Nuftt* as cared to be present.

The attendance today was unusually large. I threaded my way at Langhis' side among scores of scientists, most of them familiar to me, though not many appeared to recognize me now.

Yet as the meeting opened, I was the focus of many a sly and questioning glance.

"Be firm, my friend!" Langhis whispered, giving me

a companionable nudge. "By great Ablum! stand up for your rights!"

I clenched my fists, and gritted my teeth as I observed the hostile eyes that stared at me from all directions.

And then I heard the awaited question in the stertorous tones of Vroblis Ukko, the *Bwor* or spokesman.

"My fellow members! Is there any new resolution to consider today?"

At the extreme right of the Committee bench, a redheaded man lunged to his feet. I knew him well, the physicist Quarg Istho, with his wide slanting slit of a mouth that reminded me of a shark. Seven years ago I had competed with him for a mathematical post at Kallendra University; he had never forgiven me my victory.

"Members of the Committee! Brother scientists!" he rumbled. "I have an unhappy duty. As the latest appointee to this Committee, I was not here when you selected our representative for the *Kolem*. But like any of you, I groan when the interests of science are flouted. The gods give me the duty to propose that our representative immediately resign."

Istho paused. But before he could continue, Langhis sprang to his feet.

"My brothers! This charge is most unusual. Let the good Quarg Istho not make misty accusations. Let him state his reasons clearly."

Langhis took his seat, and Istho drew his mouth out into a long crooked slant.

"The reasons, my brothers, cannot be revealed in public. But if you knew what has come to me confidentially, you would rise and drive the culprit out like a toad. This much I can say. A great new scientific experiment has been proposed before the *Kolem* to protect the Western Isles from our enemies; and our delegate alone has opposed it. The other members of the

64

Managing Committee also have the damning facts. Is that not so, fellow members?"

I could see nods from all the Committeemen except the geologist Druz Hilo, who had voted to send me to the *Kolem*, and had been my friend from of old.

Meanwhile a fierce anger still possessed me. It was as if some outside prod had shot me to my feet. "My brothers of the *Nuftt!* I ask the honor of your attention!"

A muttering went through the gathering. But Vroblis Ukko, in his stertorous tones, assented.

"My brothers, this is not just self-defense," I proclaimed, aware of the suspicious glances from all sides. "I have tried to act for you all—for all Atlantis. Being bound by an oath of secrecy, I am like a man who speaks through suffocating veils. But I have also taken an oath to work for the good of the Western Isles. My brothers, I pray that none of you will ever have to grope through such clouds as now wrap me around. If you could see into my thoughts, you would know that I was ready to sacrifice everything personal in order to prevent an unspeakable crime."

From somewhere amid the audience, a voice cried out in challenge. "By the gods! who are you to decide what is an unspeakable crime?"

"Just one man among many," I answered, trying to keep my voice down. "Perhaps your eyes and mind are better than mine. But when I saw a move straight toward catastrophe, what would you have me do, my brothers?"

As I paused, the second Committeeman from the right was watching me wide-mouthed. But from Quarg Istho another challenge shrilled forth.

"Oh, you take the hero's pose? You're such a great man you've the right to block our national safety? How do we know you're not in the employ of the Eastern Isles?"

Keeping down my fury, I assumed a bantering tone. "That's easy to ask. And equally easy to answer, 'How do we know the Eastern Isles didn't employ you to ask that question?'"

A ripple of laughter greeted this retort.

"My brothers," I continued, "all I ask is fair play. Having thrown away nearly everything, am I to be rewarded by losing the only things still left to me—my membership in the *Kolem*—my power to fight the evil that threatens us all? Because of the enforced secrecy, you cannot have the facts. And so are you, members of the Committee, to vote in the dark, and expel me because of wild whisperings?"

As I took my seat, I could see that I had brought at least one more Committeeman to my side. But when the vote was taken, I knew that the decision was still in doubt.

The first to vote, because of his seating position, was Istho. His ringing "Yes!" for my expulsion from the *Kolem* was, of course, foreseen.

But the second voter uttered an equally ringing "No!" Then there was another "No!", then a "Yes!", and another "Yes!" One more hostile voice, and I would be out of the *Kolem*, discredited, disgraced, and defeated in all I had fought for.

The next to express himself was the third Committeeman from the left. His decision was a faltering "No," which left the tally against me three to three.

And now it was the turn of the second Committeeman to the left, in whose worn, gray face I had seen a softening. After a momentary pause, he uttered a "No!"

This made the reckoning four to three. The last voter was Druz Hilo, my old-time friend. Yet I was as one who listens in a dream when I heard his "No!"

And even while Langhis clapped me on the back in

66

congratulation, I could hardly believe that I had gained a victory in the long fight against Wauglan Waud and his band of predators.

CHAPTER XI

THE HIDDEN DAGGER STRIKES

"True, you have won a battle, Klantor. But one battle does not make a war," Langhis reminded me as we made our way together from the meeting place.

"One battle may mark the turning point in a war," I replied, expressing more confidence than I felt.

"No doubt. But there are more ways than one of getting the nuts down from a tree. Waud is an old campaigner. Truly, I *am* delighted at the results today. But I'd be blind if I were not still apprehensive."

We reached the rack where our *littos* had been parked among hundreds. "Well, Klantor, be four-eyed!" Langhis advised, meaning, "Have your wits about you!" And then, as we each started on his separate way, "I'll let you know if I see anything on the horizon."

Nearly a month later, I had been through some strenuous hours of message-carrying, and had returned to my room in the late afternoon with several messages still to deliver. As I reached a turn in the dank, dim corridor leading to my second-story lodgings, I was startled at the figure who leapt up to greet me.

"Langhis! Where in—"

"Keep your voice down! Let me in—then we'll talk!"

With shaking fingers, I turned the lock to my low-roofed, shadowy, room. I was about to step on the floor lever to switch on the light strips. But Langhis deterred me. "No! Better stay in the dark!"

"Been waiting half the afternoon," he muttered, while we stood facing one another in the gloomy half-light. "I thought you were never coming."

"But why didn't you let me know you'd be here? Or just leave a note, so I could go to you, as before?"

"I couldn't! I might never have seen you anymore!"

"Come, let's have seats," I panted, pointing to the floor cushions. "Sorry I have no *mevot* to offer you."

"As if I'm in a mood for refreshments!" he snapped, as he took the proffered seat. And then, leaning forward, "Listen, Klantor! I've news for you—again from Yonner, who knows someone connected with the Public Protectors, and has to come to me smacking his dirty lips, which have an old woman's taste for gossip. Well, the fact is Waud has filed an accusation against you."

"What, in the name of all the Isles—"

I was back on my feet, and Langhis had joined me.

"Remember what I once told you?" he answered me indirectly. "About many scientists knowing the secret of the proposed volcanic experiments? Well, again one of them has been a little loose with his tongue, though the news still hasn't broken through to the public."

"What's that to do with me?"

"Nothing on the surface. But a buzzard like Waud wouldn't be too squeamish to snatch up any piece of carrion."

I staggered a bit; tried hard to regain my balance; my head was not working well. "No—no," I answered, blankly. "I don't see."

"Someone—we don't really know who—has given out secret information supposed to concern the safety of the Western Isles. To give this out, in violation of an oath, is treason. And since you've taken your oath—"

"Oh, that's it?" I roared, an agonizing light breaking in upon me. "So he claims I've broken my oath?"

His bleak nod was answer enough.

"It's a lie! A monstrous lie!" I stormed. "I've never broken my oath!"

Langhis came to me and took my arm. "Of course, you've not broken any oath. Still, we must face the realities."

"Realities?" I demanded, savagely. "What realities?"

"Simply this, Klantor. In a world in which fraud, prejudice, and half-truth so often pass for evidence, the real question is not what you did, but what the law says you did. Under our system, you can prove anything at all so long as you have money enough for the witnesses."

I groaned. "You mean Waud will use perjured witnesses?"

"Do you doubt it? And are you forgetting whom the law prescribes as judges in trials for treason?"

In truth, I had forgotten. The court was composed of the three *Thadros* who had already, at Waud's urging, discharged me from my post at Mt. Nublis Observatory! From such political henchmen, what had I to expect?

For a moment I was silent, remembering the penalty for treason: death by poison!

"As you know," Langhis pointed out, "from a verdict of the *Thadros* there is no appeal."

"The more reason to fight it with all my power!"

"All *your* power? Tell me, what power have you?"

"Just as I fought for my rights at the *Nuftt*—"

"The *Nuftt* gave you a hearing. But this—don't you see, this would be like wrestling with an avalanche."

He laughed, shortly and harshly. And then, coming close, he spoke in low, hurried tones of suppressed emotion, "I don't have to be a prophet, Klantor, to know what will happen. Two or three Public Protectors will fall upon you—take you to a dungeon. You'll be beaten, starved, tortured. You'll be little more than a crumbled, spiritless heap of flesh by the time the trial begins. Pre-judged, pre-sentenced, what chance will you have?"

I made a throaty acknowledgement. "What can I do?"

Langhis glanced about him without answering me directly; stole over to the window, and warily peeped out.

"Yes, that's them!" he whispered, in tones that I could barely catch. "They're still there."

"Who, in great Ablum's name, is there?" I demanded, as I started toward the window.

Langhis, with an angry jerk, pulled me back. He mopped his brow, breathing heavily. "Two men— they're prowling near the outside door. I saw them when I came in. I didn't know how to get word to you, and couldn't arouse their suspicion by waiting in front. But if I went off to look for you in that maze of back alleys, you'd be sure to approach from another direction."

"As a matter of fact, I used the back entrance."

"The gods be praised for that. Now the question is: how are you to get out without ending in chains?"

This threw me into a panic. As I pictured the raw metal cutting into my limbs and choking me, I felt the terror of the hunted animal.

"How—*how can* I get out?" I cried, my defiant bravery melting away.

"You'll have to flee—leave the city—the country!" Langhis muttered. "We'll have to smuggle you out—how, I don't know. Maybe I'll get you a disguise."

"Impossible! There's no time!"

Irrelevantly, absurdly, I waved a sheaf of papers. "Besides, I've got—I've got these messages to deliver!"

"I'll see they're delivered for you!"

As in a flash of revelation, a sharp, saving thought came to me. I snatched the papers, and with much eye-strain in the dim light, picked out a certain one; then, in a fluttering voice, I blurted out my plan.

CHAPTER XII

FLIGHT

"If we can only get down to the dock, Langhis, I'm sure it will work."

"It's a desperate chance, but it just may work."

"Then let's get started! Since they're waiting in front, let's go out the back way!"

Without another word, we crept off through the twisting, narrow, ill-smelling, ill-lighted corridors. Fortunately, we met no one until, having descended one flight, we approached the rear entrance.

"Let me go first," Langhis proposed.

Well for me that he had this foresight! A minute later, while I crouched out of sight behind a turn in the corridor, he scuttled back to me, whispering excit-

73

edly, "Turn back! Two more Protectors are waiting there! Isn't there some other exit?"

"Why, yes," I answered, quickly, a daring thought flashing over me. "But it's most difficult—and dangerous. I wouldn't let any friend take such a risk for me!"

"I wouldn't let any friend take such a risk without me!"

Finding it useless to argue, I led the way to an old twisting rusted rear emergency iron staircase, which I had often noticed. Flight after flight we ascended, a full ten stories, until we stood panting on the roof. The sun, low in the sky, still gave light enough as we started across the flat, asphalt-coated surface. It was fortunate that each building in our row, like so many of the tenements, was exactly as high as its neighbors and stood against them with no intervening space.

"Faster! Faster! Faster!" some voice within me urged, as we fled across roof after roof. Always I kept looking behind me, fearing pursuit; from time to time, I stared down into the dim, narrow ravines of the streets, where people swarmed afoot or in the gliding *littos*. But before we had reached the last of the row of buildings, the sun had dipped from view beyond the city's saw-toothed skyline. Even so, we waited before daring our next move.

Groping along the roof-edge, I found one of the wire ladders that the law required as fire escapes. It would be a precarious descent—ten stories on a dangling bit of metal. "Langhis, as you love the gods," I pleaded, "you mustn't take the risk!"

"Don't waste your breath!" he chided. "Think it's dark enough yet?"

In the deep gorge of the street, all was black—we could see little except the dim outlines of the walls and an occasional gliding light.

"No use waiting," I whispered. Even as I spoke, I slipped both feet over the edge of the roof, and taking hold with my two hands on the tendril-thin wire of the ropes, began my descent.

Just then I heard a sharp ripping sound. Savagely, I gripped at the rooftop—gripped, and gained a partial hold, while the wire crumbled beneath me and my feet dangled helplessly; my hands, losing their clutch on the slippery ledge, were giving way. But I felt two strong hands closing over my arms, tugging me forward.

A moment later I was back on the roof, panting furiously, but safe!

"That wire, it's a tool of the Evil Ones!" I heard Langhis muttering. "It's not been used for years, and has rusted to a shred!"

"By great Ablum," I gasped, "you—you've saved my life!"

"Now where do we go?"

Bleakly I glanced about me. "We'll have to try some other building."

There was just enough light in the sky to show us the way to the next building. This time we did not trust the ladder until we had tested it thoroughly.

"This one seems sound as a rock," Langhis reported, after trying it with his full weight, while he clutched at the ledge for safety. "I'll go on first."

Since there was no helping it, I let him precede me. The ladder lurched and swayed frighteningly as his tall form vanished into the gloom beneath. Permitting a suitable interval to separate us, I followed; and the ladder swayed and lurched more frighteningly yet. The wires cut my hands, dug into my sandals, tormented my feet. Meanwhile, second by second, the wires seemed to grow sharper and harder to grip.

But Langhis—how was Langhis faring? The sway-

75

ing ladder showed that he still went doggedly on his way. Then at last, the ladder's end! I could just see the shadowy pavement as I let myself drop the remaining short distance.

"You clumsy calf!" a voice grumbled at my side. "You fell right on me!"

"Are you hurt, Langhis?"

"My hands are in ribbons. My feet feel as if you'd clubbed them. Otherwise, I'm splendid," he answered, drily. "And you?"

"Better than I deserve to be. Shall we keep going?"

We were in one of the pedestrian byways, one of the gulchlike depressions that ran along both sides of the street beneath the roadway, which was mostly reserved for *littos*. It was much hotter here than above, and the close air had the reek of sewage; the perspiration ran from me in streams. What was more, it was intensely dark.

We threaded our way through the cavelike depths, moving as much by touch as by sight, while in all directions the buildings towered monstrous and dark.

For a long while we went on without a word, wondering how to find the docks. We were entering a section where neither of us had ever been before: the *Hmantin*, the headquarters of robber gangs, hired thugs and assassins. Here, in a maze of twisting streets and alleys, even the Public Protectors never ventured alone.

Our feet, cut and sore from the wire ladder, ached and burned at every step. Langhis, I noticed, limped slightly. But still, by fits and spurts, we moved on, slinking along like thieves, scarcely knowing which way to turn.

"Will we never get to the docks?" Langhis mumbled, after a long time. "Or are we lost in a maze?"

"But the docks can't be far," I answered, lifting my head for an appraising sniff. Mixed with the fetid slum odors, another smell had tickled my nostrils—a pungent, fishy tang!

Langhis, I think, had caught it too; he pressed ahead with fresh energy, regardless of his hurt feet. And a glow of reflected light came to us from around the sharp turn of a street.

"The *Cruzzo!*" I cried, naming the wide avenue which, frequented at all hours, fronted on the bay.

A minute later, we came out into a blazing boulevard, where posts as tall as great trees supported horizontal strips of flat metal, longer and wider than a man's body, and glaring with an even bluish-white light. In both directions, pedestrians were moving and *littos* were flying almost as at noon; huge self-propelled freight-carrying vehicles or *onos*, like barges on rollers, were rumbling back and forth.

On the left-hand side, there were no buildings aside from sheds and warehouses. A succession of stone piers and docks occupied most of the space; and at many of the docks, ships were moored, all of the "modern" type, which one wit described as "seaworthy eggshells." They did look like enormous gray eggs: each had a convex elliptical surface, a withdrawable lookout tower, numerous hatches, and narrow wooden walks or passageways that could be pulled in during rough weather. With the hatches closed, the vessel was said to be as unsinkable as a log; it could be kept on an even keel by an internal stabilizer, and was propelled by the same volatile, alcohol-like fluid that powered the *littos*.

"Now where can we find the good vessel *Swordfish?*" I wondered, as I drew a little message paper from my pocket. And then, pointing to one of the largest craft, "Ah, blessed be the gods! There she is!"

A pang went through me—a twinge of fear—a stab of regret—a shock of foreboding mixed with remorse as I thought of my audacious scheme.

"Well, at last, Klantor, we have come to the crossroads!" sighed Langhis, with a catch in his voice.

"Don't be too sure," I answered. "If the plan doesn't work, you may have me back in a few minutes."

"I'll wait here a good time—just to make sure."

"But how will you get back home, Langhis?"

"Have no fear!" he laughed; and pointed to a sign, "*Littos* for rent."

He clapped me on the shoulder; my arm briefly enfolded him. "Here, take this—don't refuse!" he urged. And despite my protest, he forced a handful of coins upon me. "I'll be waiting by that post over there, Klantor, if you do come back. The gods be with you!"

Making a fierce effort to choke down my emotion, I crossed the gangplank to the *Swordfish*, where husky cargo carriers were trundling bales of merchandise. On the deck, an officer in a red uniform challenged me, but I waved my message paper, and he pointed along one of the wooden passageways.

A minute later, I was handing the paper to the Cargo Master, who received it with a growl and a curse. "By Ablum! this dispatch should have been here long ago, you slug! We sail at midnight!"

He did not offer me the usual messenger's fee. But my chief thought was to get away from him. I was stunned to learn that the *Swordfish* was to sail at midnight.

Uneasily I moved off along the passageway; then, after glancing warily about me, I dived into a smaller, darker passage and let myself down a hatch into a hold illuminated only with a few dim light strips.

A sailor brushed by me in the semidarkness, but evidently he mistook me for a cargo carrier. All was hot and close down here, with a sour smell. No matter! In a minute, I managed to find a crevice among the bundles and barrels of merchandise, crept in, and lay tightly wedged there, scarcely daring to breathe.

78

It seemed much later when a sudden throbbing, heaving, rolling and shuddering told me that the *Swordfish* was under way.

CHAPTER XIII

CAPTIVITY

For hours I lay half suffocated among the bales and barrels. I was desperately hot and thirsty; and it was thirst that finally brought me out, intending simply to find some water and then crawl back to my retreat.

In my half delirium, I may have moved incautiously down the dim, shuddering aisles between the piles of cargo. When I saw a spigot projecting at a bend of the aisle, and under it a basin, I went wild with eagerness. And that may be why I did not notice the two figures gliding toward me from around a turn.

"By all the isles! What have we here?"

With a shock, I looked up; looked instinctively for a place to run, but saw nowhere to go. One of the newcomers was my acquaintance, the Cargo Master, who flashed a hand torch into my eyes.

80

"May a whale swallow me! The messenger from the *Panju!*" he exclaimed, with quick recognition.

"Fins of a herring!" broke in the other man, with grating laughter. "All these stowaways are the same sort of rogues!"

"Let Captain Furzo decide what to do with him!" rattled out the Cargo Master, seizing me rudely by one arm. "Come along, you dock rat!"

Captain Furzo, whose cabin I reached after much jostling and mauling, was a square-faced redhead with two missing front teeth, a long curved scar on his left cheek, and small, cold, blue eyes that glinted suspiciously.

He received me with a snarl. "Cockroach! Don't you know the law about stowaways? We can carry them in irons back to the port they came from, before turning them over to the Public Protectors!"

Something inside me went hot and cold by turns.

Furzo surveyed me with a long doubtful glance of his evil glinting little eyes. "We're shorthanded in the lower cargo holds!" he growled. "If we don't put you in chains, you sneaking weasel, think you could show a strong arm down there?"

"I'd work like a pack mule."

"So they all say! But if you don't do more than three other men, the chains are still here!"

He slapped his knee in mirth; then bawled at one of the men, "Down with him to sub-hold A!"

Never before had I visited such a den. The air was sour, rancid, musty, and hot. The cargo, piled to the ceiling along the sloping bulkheads in the eerie glow of amber wall strips, was constantly shifting; and it was my duty to lash it down with ropes and wires. This task, even in clean, cool air, would have been strenuous; in the semidarkness of the heaving deck, with a master cracking a whip over my shoulders, it was the bitterest slavery.

81

I hardly knew how much time went by. Each day was an unending ordeal. At each day's close I was somehow able to force down my unappetizing gruel and throw myself down on my straw for a few hours' nightmare-broken sleep.

A single brief release was granted me: once every day, when the sea was calm, I might climb to the deck for a few minutes of the reviving fresh air. Only then could my tormented mind ask questions. Where was I going? Could I slip away when we reached port? Or would I be returned to Kallendra and my enemies?

Thinking of my escape and of the *Kolem*, I groaned. Another, I knew, would be appointed in my place and permit Wauglan Waud's infamous experiment to destroy the fairest of the Cocoanut Isles. And this in time, I still dreaded, would lead to still more terrible destruction.

But someday, perhaps, I would return to Kallendra, and would still deal a blow to Waud and his kind. Someday I *must* return; only in Kallendra could I find Lampra again.

From the beginning, my hope had been to steal away at the first port. But had my captors read my mind? Time after time, the rolling and heaving of the vessel ceased, and I heard instead a variety of telltale noises: thumpings and bumpings, shouts and other harbor sounds. But always I was sealed in the reeking gloom of sub-hold A.

As a famished man dreams of food, I dreamt of escape. I thought of a thousand schemes, all of which, upon examination, appeared worthless. The brutal eyes of Captain Furzo or of the Cargo Master or his underlings, were upon me constantly. And then at one port, whose name I did not even know, I saw a gleam of hope.

Even in the depths of the hold, I heard a tremendous splash, followed by yells and cries, which were minutes in dying down. Then a port burst open above me, and the burly form of the Cargo Master stood framed in the feeble light. "Come, you slimy eel!" he yelled.

I started forward, and the Cargo Master barked at a long-armed spider of a man. "Monl Jung! Take charge of the worm! By all the shrimps of the Nine Seas! if that crazy gangplank hadn't broken and drowned those other scamps, I wouldn't call on this scrap of scum! We've got to get away by the third hour of the night! We need every work animal! Keep the whip on his flank!"

Monl Jung, whom I knew only too well (my arms, shoulders, and chest bore his whip marks) snapped a lash in my face. "Into sub-hold B!" he commanded. "Start moving those bales and boxes onto the dock!"

In line with a dozen other men, I began hauling crates so huge that I staggered beneath their weight. From the upper deck I gazed in fascination at the port: Three snow-packed mountains dominated the distance; and on their lower slopes, beneath dense green forests, the city curved gracefully, with rainbow-colored domes, turrets, and pagodas.

But of all this I had only a glimpse. Tugging and groaning, I crossed the gangplank and dropped my burden among stacks of merchandise. In all directions, I saw a vast rush and activity, porters and messengers dashing back and forth, cargo-carriers entering and leaving the ships, and self-propelled *onos* arriving on the granite-paved streets and bearing away the goods.

As I put down my load, I glanced about me furtively, hoping for a chance to dash away. But Monl Jung's whip swiftly disillusioned me.

Trip after trip I made into the reeking hold of the *Swordfish*. Soon I was aching in every limb. But my

83

mind remained alert—and well that it did! The glare of day was just giving place to twilight when, as I came down the gangplank, stooping beneath my thirtieth load, I saw a man in a gray uniform approach a green stone column, throw open a little panel, and turn a switch. As he closed the panel, hundreds of blue-white light strips began shining from posts above.

At this, a wild scheme took shape in my mind. The first hour of the night came, and the second, and the excitement on the *Swordfish* grew. "Get a move on, you mud-fish!" Monl Jung kept yelling at me, not sparing the whip. "Don't you know we leave at the third hour?"

But Jung had other workers to watch, and this gave me my opportunity. The third hour was already approaching when I put one load more down on the dock and, pausing to regain my breath, was unable to see Jung anywhere. My immediate impulse was to run away. But I feared that someone would give the alarm, and I would be recaptured. No! I had a better plan.

Even as I made my decision, I saw Jung eyeing me suspiciously from the top of the gangplank. But this only sped my feet. Impetuously I dashed the dozen paces to the green stone column, threw open a little panel, and turned a switch. All at once the world went black.

CHAPTER XIV

A THRUST FOR FREEDOM

There was a startled half second of silence. Then, from all about me, I heard shouts, yells, shrieks, oaths, and growls of profanity. A woman screamed. Some-one clamored in terror. Here and there, in the dis-tance, I saw the firefly stab of an electric torch.

Meanwhile, losing not an instant, I carried out my plan. Less than twenty paces away, I had seen a wooden crate, taller than a man, which stood with its side half open; within it, there was a gray plastic bag, and between the bag and the wall of the crate there was just enough space to squeeze into. I had carefully noted the position of the crate, in the middle of the dock at the end of a row of great boxes; by feeling my way, I was able to find it in the darkness.

Hardly had I shut myself inside when I heard a

roar, followed by a cheer, and saw light shining through a needle-thin chink in the crate lid. As I had expected, the authorities had turned an emergency switch.

Inside the crate, I was so cramped that I could hardly breathe. But if I could only hold out a little while, the *Swordfish* would sail, and I could escape!

Then, from just outside, a bellowing jarred upon my ears.

"That's it, boys! Look hard and fast! It's an extra five days' wages for any of you who catches him!"

"When we've taught him his lesson," snarled a second speaker, "he'll have more stripes on his body than hairs on his head! Over there, men, in that heap of sacks!"

The voices drew further away; were lost amid the commotion of the port. Then once more I heard a familiar snarl.

"Now where could that worm have crawled? Hurry, boys! Look in those boxes over there! I've a feeling in my shins that beast is near us right now!"

My crate shook as the searchers brushed against it. I heard them cursing and swearing; my heart was pounding furiously. Then suddenly it gave a leap. I felt a violent jerk, the crate turned over on one side, and I found myself lying face down, struggling for air. Then the crate turned again; I felt it bobbing up and down, as if being carried.

So my ruse had been discovered! Imprisoned inside the crate, I was being carted back to the *Swordfish*!

Such was my despairing conclusion. But the voices just outside were unfamiliar, in an odd dialect never heard on our isle of Xandu.

"Scaly lizards!" a disagreeable voice grumbled. "I've never known them make these crates so heavy before!"

"It's a dirty plot to make us poor fellows do twice

86

the work for the same pay!" growled a second voice.

At the same time, I felt a rocking motion, then was jarred and jolted by the hardest thump of all. The crate had come to rest on a solid surface.

And there for some time it lay, while I heard a succession of thuds and crashes as of crates being piled above me. Then I felt rolling, grinding, and crunching beneath me, and recognized the truth I had half suspected: my crate had been thrown on an *ono*, one of the self-propelled freight vehicles, on its way to some unknown destination!

For a mercilessly long while we rolled and jolted forward. I tried to raise the top lid, but evidently other crates rested above. Finally, after many stops, starts, and shocks, the rolling, grinding, and crunching ceased. On all sides, I heard a pounding and banging, accompanied by oaths and curses; then felt my crate being lifted and slammed down on end. Ill and weak and numbed, I waited until all the sounds had ceased, then lifted the lid and painfully crept out.

In the dim artificial light, I could see that I was in an enormous shed, where my crate had been left in line with numerous others. Above it there was a rack filled with boxes and bags, and above this there was still another rack; and similar racks, likewise packed with merchandise, stared from across a wide aisle.

By the pallid yellowish glow from the light strips on the arched ceiling many yards above, I was just able to read the inscription on my crate. No wonder that the Cargo Master and his men had not looked for me here! A sign, in large purple letters on one side of the crate, bore the notation: "DANGER! Poison! Rat spray!"

My limbs were now so cramped and bruised that I could hardly walk. My head was aching; my nerves felt pounded by battering rams. Seeing some old sacks lying on the floor in an aisle between rows of barrels, I was barely able to drag my way to them for some badly needed sleep.

I had no idea how much time went by, when from somewhere not far off there came an immense crashing. As I struggled to my feet, moved out from between the rows of barrels, and glanced down the main aisle, I saw a wedge of sunlight shining from what I took to be the direction of the entrance.

At the same time, I noticed a large sign dangling from the ceiling:

KIMPOC WAREHOUSE NUMBER 1
Trespassing is forbidden by the Anti-Vagrancy Law. Violators will be turned over to the Public Protectors.

Having no desire for a brush with the Public Protectors, I started off as fast as my bruised, stiff body permitted.

But I had gone not a dozen paces when two men popped up from around a mountain of piled boxes— burly fellows, dressed in brown-striped tunics such as I had never seen before, their reddish hair done up in knots in a style quite new to me.

"By the great god Quabbu! Who have we here?" one of them coughed at me, with a foreign accent.

"Maybe you didn't read that sign over there?" snapped the second, pointing. "Can't you tramps get it into your thieving heads everything worth taking here is locked up? Now will you tell me why we shouldn't call the Protectors?"

"There's nothing, my friends, to call the Protectors about," I answered, in my suavest tones. "I didn't come here to take anything except a job."

They both roared.

"Those fancy party clothes of yours," one of them gibed, pointing to my tunic, which was ripped, rav-

88

elled, soiled, and begrimed, "where did you ever get them? Well, better come along!"

One of the pair lunged forward and grabbed me. But I kicked and fought with a fierceness I hardly knew I was capable of. For several minutes the scuffle raged on, bringing a rush of witnesses, one of them a tall, hook-nosed, commanding-looking man in a maroon-colored tunic. He at once took control; called off the assailants, and yelled, "Bruttl! What's the fight all about?"

"Well, by the gods, Master Kimpoc," one of my attackers explained, meekly, "this man's a vagabond."

Master Kimpoc cast me a searching glance of his glittering gray falcon's eyes.

"Bruttl," he flung back, scornfully, "you may be a good hand at checking freight, but the gods did not qualify you as a judge of human beings. Can't you look into this man's face and see that he is no vagabond?" Then sharply, to me, while half a dozen onlookers stood about, listening: "Who are you, sir?"

"I'll be glad to explain," I answered, quickly. "But not with an army of witnesses leaning over my shoulders."

Kimpoc cast me another scrutinizing glance.

"You do not talk like a native of Klatchen," he diagnosed.

So I was in Klatchen, the chief of the Eastern Isles!

"This way!" he motioned. And soon I was seated opposite him on a pile of cushions in a little office.

"What's your name?"

"Munjin Alg."

"Munjin Alg? I once knew an Alg, from the Western Isles. From your way of speech I would say you too, are from those unfortunate parts."

"You're a keen judge," I answered. "I am truly from the Western Isles. I came quite against my will. In my own land, I occupied a respectable position. But not

89

long ago, on a cursed wager, a friend and I visited the *Hmantin* district of Kallendra—maybe you've heard of it—"

My interviewer gave a disgusted twist to his broad, heavy lips.

"The two of us," I rushed on, "were wandering through the *Hmantin*, picking up local color, when we were attacked by thugs. My friend, thanks to the gods! escaped. But I was kidnapped, thrown aboard a vessel, and made to work like a slave. Luckily, I broke away on reaching here."

"What was the ship's name?"

"The *Swordfish.*"

"Ah, yes," reflected Kimpoc, leaning back on his pile of cushions and stroking his down-pointing red mustache. "I know the leaky old cask. But how did you get away?"

I described my experience in the crate of rat spray, and Kimpoc laughed.

"If you really were kidnapped," he concluded, "you can thank the gods you got away to a good country. What do you intend doing now?"

"First of all, I want a job."

"Well," he reflected, leaning far back against the blue-panelled wall and still regarding me quizzically, "we have ten warehouses in the Kimpoc chain—biggest business of the kind in all Admenebda."

I gasped. Admenebda was the capital and greatest seaport of the Eastern Isles—a city of several millions, which I had always heard described as an abyss of iniquity.

"We employ many men," Kimpoc went on, still scrutinizing me intently, "but one of your type would be of little use to move cargo from the docks or pile it on our racks here." He hesitated briefly. "However, there's one service where—but no, you'd never do in the Computation Department."

90

I shot forward in my seat. "That sounds right in my field! You see," I went on, again improvising, "at Kallendra, I worked for an engineering firm."

"Oh! Well, this job is not quite like engineering. We have to figure such things as volume and shape of storage areas, what can be stored most efficiently. Sometimes it's more complicated than a snarled cable."

I laughed. "That doesn't alarm me."

"So they all say—at first. However"— Kimpoc arose suddenly, and I did likewise—"come back tomorrow at this time. I'll have a problem for you. Take all day to work it out. If you succeed, the job is yours. Meanwhile," he threw out, with a glance at my ragged apparel, "have you the means to exist?"

"I have some money—Western Isle money."

He shook his head. "You can't pass that here. I'll change it for you into good Eastern currency."

"Looking for a place to live?" he continued. "Then go to your left the length of this street. At the far end you'll see the Wayfarers' Hotel—not a bad place. Tomorrow morning, then!"

The Wayfarers' Hotel, for a modest fee, offered me a pleasing room. And I arranged to take my meals at the same establishment.

After several hours' rest, I wandered abroad into the city's main sections. The people, as they swarmed past, were so much like our own Kallendrans that I would have seen no difference at all, had it not been for their tiger-striped and leopard-spotted tunics and their unique headdresses. Noticing how they laughed, chattered, and frolicked, I could not see in them the relentless savages who, I had been taught, populated the Eastern Isles.

The city also astonished me; it surpassed even Kallendra, which, I had been told, was the world's most resplendent city. The streets were wide and had flow-

91

ered patches in the center. For a small fee, I rented a *litto*; and I saw that in the middle-class residential sections all the avenues were delightfully curved and tree-lined. In Kallendra, only persons of wealth could enjoy such accommodations.

Promptly at the agreed time next morning, I returned to the warehouse, expecting some difficult mathematical problem. But the test was so simple that, with my experience at complex calculations, I worked less than an hour over the questions.

"By Quabbu! I wouldn't call you a novice!" Kimpoc commended, a gleam of admiration in his shining falcon's eyes. "Really, you will be wasted in our Computation Department. But if you want to join us, you can begin today."

CHAPTER XV

A BOLT FROM THE WESTERN ISLES

"Doubtless, Munjin Alg, you'd feel happier in Eastern costume," remarked my employer, after a day or two. "Here! I'll advance the money from your salary." Hence I was soon clad in a parrot-green tunic, of a style popular in Admenebda.

This was but one of his many favors to me. Several times he increased my wages; more important yet, he befriended me personally. We had many long talks, and constantly he urged me to remain in the Eastern Isles.

Then one day he invited me to his home, on a street fragrant with jasmine and blooming lemon trees. There I was hospitably received by his wife Chantrun and his three daughters, all of them charming girls, though the most charming of all was the eldest, Olamul, a dancing-eyed, coppery-haired creature of twenty, who reminded me of Lampra.

How easy it would have been to form an attachment with her! When she leaned toward me, smiling out of her live, dark eyes, I would have been blind not to read the encouragement in her glance, and blind not to see that her parents were piling no obstacles between us. Yes, had I been a different man, how easy to rebuild my life!

And yet—and yet I knew it all an impossible dream. I could not turn my back upon Lampra; I could not put her out of my mind, though few things were more unlikely than that I would ever see her again. Would I really be untrue to her if I did embrace another, now that she was cut off from me forever? So temptation whispered; but always I would hear in my mind the words of Lampra, her sorrowful last message, ". . . be of good cheer, my best beloved. Surely the gods, being good, will bring us together again. . . ."

Somewhere, I felt, she was still waiting, in the faith that the gods would indeed bring us together again.

But do not think my decision easy. Being a man, with all a man's full-grown impulses, needs, and longings, I found it agonizingly hard to give up the radiant, visible Olamul for a Lampra who was fast growing more ghostly. I cannot say—since no man knows himself to the depths—how long my strength would have held out had I continued to visit her home.

But fate was preparing another sharp about-face in my fortunes. One day, while I was at work in the office, Kimpoc made a chance remark that was to have portentous effects.

"Oh, by the way, Munjin, you'll be interested in this. One of your dignitaries will be stopping off here in a day or two, and be given a great reception by our *Magnonem*."

I looked up from a sheet filled with computations. The *Magnonem*, I knew, was the head of the ruling oligarchy of the Eastern Isles. But I felt no interest in him or his receptions.

"What's the visitor's name?" I asked.

"By Quabbu, I'm not much good at remembering these Western names. It's something like—well, like Amdrillon—no, more like Amgillon—"

As if he had struck me, I shot to my feet.

"It couldn't," I demanded, "be Argillon?"

"Yes, by the gods, that sounds right."

I circled about the room; tried not to let him see my agitated face. But his falcon's eyes were following me, and I expected the inquiry that he flung at me, "Anybody, Munjin, that you happen to know?"

"Yes, truly—somebody I do happen to know."

"As one of your ruling body, he'll be received with official honors," my employer went on. "He's coming on what they call a friendship tour."

After all, it was really not strange that Argillon, as an emissary of the West, should visit the capital of the Eastern Isles. But he had not gone on his cruise alone!

"Maybe, my friend, you'd like to see him. But there's no way I know of. He'll be guarded by a big corps of Public Protectors; all tickets to the reception will be by special invitation. However," Kimpoc went on, "just before the reception, he is to make a brief talk to our people in the *Mjana*, our central square. If you'd care to listen, by Quabbu, you may have time off work."

"I'd like that very much," I assented. For where Argillon was, there Lampra also would be! And if, even for one swift stolen moment—

But one swift stolen moment would not be enough. Here, surely, was my chance, the opportunity I had fervently awaited! If I could get word to her, arrange

95

a rendezvous—then I might tear her from beneath her father's very eyes, and we might flee together!

Such was my dream. Yet the obstacles were mountainous. I could not approach Lampra by ordinary means; and it would be too dangerous to attempt to reach her by the public messenger service at the *Prajn* or Hotel for Notables, where she would stay; any communication would be intercepted. Clearly, I myself must place the letter in Lampra's hands.

But how could I? I inquired into the arrangements for Argillon's address; and found that he was to appear on a platform in the *Mjana*, along with his daughter and a reception committee. But I could not possibly reach Lampra on the platform. Before arriving there, however, the members of the party would have to walk half the width of the *Mjana* (about a hundred paces). My one chance, therefore, was while Lampra was covering this distance afoot. With swiftness and daring, I might press a message into her hands.

Carefully I planned the message, going over the words time after time in my mind. Only after much rewriting did I contrive the following:

> *Precious One:*
> *Do not be surprised to find me in the Eastern Isles. All is well. I have never forgotten. My loyalty and love have never wavered. I have been waiting for our hour. Now it is at hand. Meet me tonight at the fourth hour just outside the side entrance of the* Prajn. *One bold stroke—and all is won!*
> *In eternal devotion,*
>
> *Klantor*

At the end of the message, I placed our little secret symbol: "X * * X."

I had plotted everything so well that the plans, I

96

was certain, must succeed. Lampra would surely contrive to meet me at the fourth hour tonight outside her hotel. There I would have two hired *littos* waiting, and we would rush to a *dardo*, an official entitled to perform marriage ceremonies; and he, who would be expecting us, would give us a ticket of temporary admission to the *Kra-leld*, Municipal Bridal Quarters, where we would stay until we could make other arrangements. There even Argillon would be powerless against us.

How excitedly, on the day of Argillon's promised address, I made my way to the *Mjana!* In one hand, while I ranged about impatiently, I clutched something more precious than gold—my message to Lampra. After a time, I saw that a pathway two or three paces wide, leading from the platform to the outskirts of the *Mjana*, was being cut off from the public by heavy wire ropes; I pressed as near to the wires as I could.

Meanwhile, my attention was drawn to the other onlookers, most of them young, many of them with morose, smoldering eyes and a frowning fierceness of aspect. Some held objects in their hands, but I could not make out just what they were. I was surprised to find the crowd composed nine tenths of men.

After a long while, the ceremonies seemed about to begin. The purple-and-green flag of the Western Isles, raised on a flagpole beside the yellow-and-black banners of the Eastern Isles, was greeted by faint cheers from some quarters, but by hisses from the men and women all around me.

Now a corps of Public Protectors, resplendent in gold and crimson, marched down the central aisle, and waved the people back from the wire ropes. Then there came a blare of trumpets, followed by an awed silence from the thousands of spectators. And I knew that the crisis was at hand.

97

"We greet a distinguished visitor from the Western Isles," a voice droned from the sound machine on the platform. "He comes on a mission of friendship, to seal the bonds between our two mighty empires. Bow low, citizens of Admenebda! Bow low to Argillon, second in rank of the *Kolem* of the Western Isles!"

Again there were cheers and hisses.

On a surge of pushing, squeezing bodies, I was shoved painfully against the ropes, from which the swords of the Protectors drove us back. A tumult of cries was in my ears as a line of dignitaries drew near, clad in velvety yellow-fringed black, and escorting a tall figure whom I instantly recognized. Argillon glanced neither to right nor to left; his chilly blue eyes were like those of some arrogant king.

Then, just behind him and his escort, I observed a flash of royal blue as a party of ladies came swishing forward. And walking a little apart from this group, I saw *her*. Clad in a swirl of snow-white, an emerald headdress crowning her coppery curls, she came forward slowly, a bit paler than of old, but more beautiful than ever. She was looking to one side, and apparently did not see me.

Now was the time to act. Clutching my message, I pressed against the wire ropes. A few seconds, and Lampra would be within touching distance, and I would dart the message into her hands.

Like an athlete poised to leap, I crouched low. And then the world exploded into pandemonium.

From just beyond me, where Argillon had passed with his party, shouts, yells, and catcalls burst forth; cries of "Down with the Western Islers! Death to the betrayers!" There was a clattering of stones, a rattling of swords. A scream of terror shrilled forth as the mob surged forward. Men and women, their faces contorted, were lifting their arms and throwing heavy objects; I heard the crashing of clods and rocks. With a

98

savage jerk, I lunged forward, and caught the arm of a man who was aiming a stone at Lampra. The stone thudded down harmlessly; I had barely a glimpse of the girl's distended face before a bevy of Public Protectors clattered about her and hid her from view. All the while, I still clutched the message, whose top had been torn away.

"Down with the Westerners! Death to the betrayers!" clamored the mob; while, beaten and mauled, my left cheek bleeding from the glancing blow of a rock, I tried to force my way out of the rabble.

Then suddenly I realized my peril. Swiftly I was surrounded. Gold-and-crimson tunics flashed all about me; swords gleamed; triple-headed pikes glinted in the sunlight. Too late, I saw the Public Protectors cut off a pushing, squirming knot of rioters, in whose center I was tightly wedged.

Like a man who watches the unraveling of preordained doom, I heard a clanking of chains; I saw fettered men writhing; and in a reckless last effort, I struggled to work my way free. But two chain-wielding giants bore down upon me, and I felt the bite of steel about my wrists.

CHAPTER XVI

TRIAL AND JUDGMENT

"By Quabbu, get into there, you snakes! If any of
you so much as opens his verminous mouth, we'll
have his head on a pole!"

Swinging their long pikes, the Public Protectors
herded their prisoners into a gray brick courtyard enclosed by tall spike-crowned walls. The larger part
was open to the sky, but one end held a series of
sheds equipped with filthy straw mats. In the open
space, a hundred or more men were sitting, standing
or lying—most of them torn and ragged, some badly
scarred, and all bearing on their wrists the indenta-
tions of chains.

Our own chains, to my great relief, were unlocked
when we entered the enclosure. At the same time, one

100

of the guards snatched from me the pathetic remains of that message to Lampra.

As I slumped down upon the brick pavement, it was hard for me to realize the extent of the calamity. Could I actually be under arrest—under arrest for molesting Lampra? I groaned at the irony; this was all part of the sardonic destiny that had been pursuing me. The words of the Seeress of the Dawn came back, and came back, "Small storms precede great! Small storms precede great! Small storms precede great!"

I was startled out of my broodings by a voice at my side. "The gods want to punish us, brother. Else they wouldn't have tripped up our plans."

I looked up into a youthful face, with two blood-shot eyes, and a pinched, haggard look.

"Surely, the gods do want to punish us."

"The fault is not of the gods—no, by all the isles!" dissented a weedy youth with a twist in his face. "We acted too fast. We didn't all work together. If we had been more skilled, that gray wolf from the Western Isles and his slut of a daughter would have had a gift to remember us by!"

"His daughter is no slut!" I denied, indignantly.

A third man—a stooping colossus with a bull-like face and large bulging bull's eyes—had sauntered up. "I say the only good Western Islander is a dead one," he rumbled. "It's my belief they sent this Argillon and his siren of a daughter as spies to ferret out our secrets."

"Why is it," snapped the weedy youth, "that we few patriots were the only ones arrested, when at least five hundred were protesting?"

"Didn't they have to arrest somebody?" growled the bull-faced one. "For the sake of diplomatic relations with those bandits in the West, they have to punish the ringleaders."

"But we're not ringleaders!"

"So what?" argued the man with the bloodshot eyes. "Somebody has to be accused!"

, Just then a trio of sword-bearing jailors strode toward us, carrying papers and writing sticks, which they distributed among the new-made captives. "Here, you scorpions—your questionnaire!" one of them snapped. "By Quabbu! answer truly, if you don't want to sleep in the Black Pit!"

Most of the queries—name, age, address, father's name, occupation, etc.—were easy to answer. But I did not know how to state my political affiliations, and I left the space blank. Again, I was puzzled at the notation: "References: name at least two, preferably more." Of course, I put down the name of my employer Kimpoc; but there I had to stop, since he was my only acquaintance in the Eastern Isles aside from the members of his family.

Meanwhile, might I not send Kimpoc a message, notifying him of my plight, and soliciting his aid? But when I put this question to one of the jailors, the man stared at me as if I had asked his right arm.

"What! send a message, you insolent scrap of carrion!" he snarled. "Do you think we're running a coddling place for criminals?"

Ominously his sword clanked against its scabbard.

Ten dreary days later, the trial was held. One morning we were startled by the tolling of a bell high up on one of the spiked stone walls. Then a sonorous voice burst forth: "The following suspects will proceed at once to the gate!" And while the hundred or more prisoners stood, sat, or lay stockstill in awed silence, a list of names came forth with a slow and portentous intonation.

There were twenty in all, but the one I awaited was not among them. The end of the list had seemingly been reached; the speaker paused; then, with a wildly thumping heart, I heard him resume: "Munjin Alg."

As I joined the line before the gate, rows of guards with brandished swords began shepherding us through long winding galleries to a great hall. There rising above us to more than a man's height, stood a platform with copper railings and three damasked copper-red chairs. Each chair supported a bulky figure with an official black velvet tunic and an air of godlike aloofness. All three were old and wrinkled, with stern, set faces.

But as my gaze wandered from the judges to the spectators waiting in the semicircular rows of seats, I had a shock of glad surprise. Smiling reassuringly at me, my friend and employer Kimpoc was seated in the first row. Since I had given his name as a reference, the authorities had advised him of the trial.

At this realization, new hope blazed up. Kimpoc, naturally, knew that I was innocent. Surely he would know how to get me free!

With the deep, hollow pealing of a gong, the proceedings began. Even as the notes died down, a fat man in a black tunic waddled to the judges' platform, bared a lance-wielding jasper figure, and bent low.

"O Quabbu! Great god of the Eastern Isles!" he prayed. "O patron deity of our superb city of Admenebda! I, your humble priest, beg of you, help us to further our ideal! Peace, honor, and right! Mercy, justice, and light!"

As the priest lumbered away, his corpulent frame puffing, the tones were taken up and chanted by hundreds of voices. "Peace, honor, and right! Mercy, justice, and light!"

At the same time, my attention was drawn to a spot midway between the benches and the judges' platform; a trapdoor had opened in the floor and a smaller platform had risen to a height a few feet below that of the judges. Up a stairway on this second platform, a tall and lean, angular man gingerly climbed.

103

"Droon Dundruhu, the Public Denouncer!" whispered the prisoner to my right.

Waving his immense arms above his silvery tunic, Dundruhu stood on the newly erected platform, by turns looking up at the judges and down at us prisoners. He bowed briefly, then began speaking from a throat that seemed made of solid brass.

"Brothers and sisters of the Eastern Isles! We are here today to pass judgment on some vicious offenders. For many years, as you know, the policy of our Government has been peace with the Western Isles! We have bent nearly double; we have prostrated ourselves almost to the ground to Kallendra's treacherous and unpredictable rulers. When they recently sent one of their leading men on a mission of friendship, some of our citizens began hurling hisses and missiles at the distinguished visitor. Their acts were subversive. Fortunately, our honored visitor and his daughter escaped injury. But the incident has stirred up a storm in the Western Isles, which can be quieted only if we make an example of some of the worst offenders."

Dundruhu paused, and glared at us prisoners. But I was mightily relieved in one way. Now I knew that Lampra had not been hurt.

Then, from the bench above, there came the drone of the white-bearded judge. "Let us proceed to cases!"

The Public Denouncer drew a long green-bordered paper from a recess of his tunic, and read, "We begin with the charge against Oon Truigin!"

"Oon Truigin! Stand up!"

The prisoner with the bloodshot eyes arose tremblingly. His head was bowed, and his knees shook.

"Oon Truigin!" thundered the Public Denouncer. "You are charged with treason, and inspiring to riot, insurrection, and rebellion. Do you take your oath, by

104

the sacred name of Quabbu, to answer all questions truly and honestly?"

"I take my oath—by the sacred name of Quabbu."

Hundreds of spectators were leaning forward expectantly.

"Did you, or did you not, inspire to riot, insurrection, and rebellion?"

"I—I—by the gods, yes," the prisoner answered, in quavering tones.

"Have you any excuse for such criminal conduct?"

"No, Your Eminence. No excuse, except—except that I acted in patriotism, from love of our dear Eastern Isles."

"That will be all, Oon Truigin!" blared Droon Dundruhu. "The noble judges will now decide the case!"

Truigin fell back rather than sat down on the bench. A minute's silence followed, while the "noble judges" whispered and conferred.

"Oon Truigin, stand up for sentencing!"

Oon Truigin did not exactly stand; he was supported by the arms of two fellow sufferers, while in severe tones the judge announced the verdict.

"It is most serious for a private citizen to disturb international relations by insulting and attacking a foreign official. Oon Truigin, we sentence you for one year to Project J!"

Truigin groaned, and sank back upon the bench.

"What's Project J?" I whispered to the prisoner to my left.

He muttered and shook his head. With monotonous regularity, case after case was disposed of. Everybody admitted his guilt; but everybody swore to the purest patriotic motives.

As the trial proceeded, my own hopes dwindled. I was almost in despair when at last I heard two awaited words: "Munjin Alg!"

"Plead guilty. That's the one road to an easy sentence," whispered the prisoner to my left. But something within me rebelled as the Public Denouncer stood on his platform, pointing a long, thin, condemning finger in my direction.

"Munjin Alg! You are charged with treason! Do you take your oath, by the sacred name of Quabbu?"

"I take my oath—by the sacred name of Quabbu."

"Noble Judges! Brothers and sisters of the Eastern Isles!" Dundruhu declaimed, turning with an oratorical gesture to the judges, and then to the audience. "I have left the case of Munjin Alg to the last for I have reason to suspect that we have here one of the infamous leaders of the conspiracy to provoke trouble with the Western Isles. This evidence I shall place before you. First, however, a question for the prisoner!"

He paused, and that long, thin, condemning finger seemed to point straight at my heart.

"Munjin Alg! Answer simply and honestly! Did you not participate in a conspiracy to inspire to riot, insurrection, and rebellion?"

"No, Your Eminence!"

A low murmuring swept the audience. From somewhere in the rear, there came a sound as of a hundred cats hissing. But an approving glitter lighted the gray falcon's eyes of my friend Kimpoc.

"What's that, you double-faced fox?" the Public Denouncer roared at me, "You have the effrontery to deny your guilt? By Quabbu! How comes it, then, that you were in the very heart of the rioters?"

"A mere unlucky chance, Your Eminence," I defended, trying to make myself heard above the undercurrent of hisses. "Far from wanting to harm the visitors, I stopped a rioter from hurling a stone at Lamp—at Argillon's daughter."

"Holy name of the *Magnonem!*" gibed the Public

106

Denouncer. "You take us for fools. Where are your witnesses?"

Of course, I could mention no witnesses. And the hall, consequently, was swept by scornful laughter.

"Now, Munjin Alg," Dundruhu blazed on, as he reached for several papers, which were passed to him from below by a red-braided page, "here is the questionnaire you signed in prison. You were asked for two or more references. But you mentioned only one. What do you expect us to believe of a man who can name only one person to say a word for him?"

I opened my mouth to reply. But the Public Denouncer rushed on.

"Now for a still more serious matter! When asked to state your political affiliations, you left the space blank. What does this mean, Munjin Alg?"

"Your Eminence, I have no political affiliations."

Again laughter, accompanied by hisses.

"By Quabbu! even the lowest thief has political affiliations! Noble judges! form your own conclusions. What would a man claim if he belonged to a secret organization, which aimed at subversion and international turmoil?"

The judges nodded.

"And now for the most damning evidence," the Denouncer blustered on, waving a rumpled scrap of paper that, somehow, seemed familiar. "Here we have a document found on the prisoner. With the guile common to his class, he tore off the top, which doubtless contained the most incriminating data of all. However, what is left is eloquent enough. Noble judges, let me read it to you!"

Were these my own words that were being read? ". . . . I have never forgotten. My loyalty and love have never wavered. I have been waiting for our hour. Now it is at hand. Meet me tonight at the fourth hour just outside the side entrance of the *Prajn*. One bold stroke—and all is won. In eternal devotion. Klantor."

A long, deep-throated jeer, arising far back in the audience, spread swiftly through the hall.

" 'Klantor,' " Dundruhu proclaimed, in his brassy voice, "is clearly an assumed name. The rest of the message is easy to see through. 'My loyalty and love' of course means, 'my loyalty and love for the insurrection.' The same with, 'I have never forgotten' . . . 'waiting for our hour.' All this, plainly, refers to the treasonous plot. It is my theory that an assassination attempt was afoot."

The Denouncer brought his fist down emphatically. During the ensuing pause, a wave of boos travelled through the audience, followed by fresh hisses.

"Here, noble judges," Dundruhu hurried on, "is even more convincing evidence. At the bottom of the page, there is a cryptic symbol—an X followed by three stars and another X. Our coding specialists have been trying for days to fathom the meaning. So I ask you, exalted judges, why would the writer resort to a secret code?"

The judges shook their heads solemnly. New boos and hisses shuddered through the audience. But I did, in my indignation, manage to make myself heard.

"Your Eminence! I would never under the stars plot against the Western Isles. I myself am a Western Islander. As for the message—and the symbol of the X followed by the stars—it is a mere lovers' device—"

Laughter, gathering to a roar, burst upon me in a blast that drowned out my words.

Then once more the Public Denouncer raised his stertorous voice. "Noble judges! Does the accused consider this court a jesting place? Am I expected to believe that a battlefield of rioters was really a lovers' alcove?"

After fresh laughter, the prosecutor continued.

"Munjin Alg! Come, tell us, who is this Klantor—this writer of loving notes? Who is his dear lady?"

Again I saw Dundruhu's long condemning finger pointed at me; again I saw the amused and derisive looks in hundreds of pairs of eyes. I knew that I was hopelessly trapped.

"A sacred obligation binds me not to mention the lady's name," I pleaded.

"Noble judges," the Public Denouncer roared on, "the prisoner has relieved me of the duty of saying much more. As for his claim to come from the Western Isles—that is, on the face of it, too preposterous to be worth discussing."

"Your Eminence!" a strong voice interrupted from the front semicircle of seats as a tall, hook-nosed man in a maroon-colored tunic sprang to his feet. "I ask the privilege of just a word!"

A startled silence followed. Every eye was turned upon the speaker's dominating figure.

"Assuredly, Master Kimpoc," deferentially acknowledged the Denouncer, to whom Kimpoc, as one of the city's leading businessmen, was well known. "Do you take your oath in the name of Quabbu?"

"In the name of Quabbu, I take my oath!"

A brief hope shot through me as I stared gratefully at Kimpoc's serene, commanding figure.

"A great mistake has been made," Kimpoc proclaimed, in a full, rich voice. "For some time Munjin Alg has been in my service, and a more capable employee I have never had. He could not have planned to join in the riot, for he did not know of the coming of the Western Islanders until a day or two in advance. Besides, he tells the truth in claiming to be from the Western Isles. My business, which brings me into contact with men from many lands, has taught me to distinguish the peculiar Western intonation."

"But, Master Kimpoc!" the Denouncer dissented,

sharply, "any good actor could imitate it. Have you any other witness? The law says there must be two. If there are not, it can take no account of your testimony."

"Hear me, noble judges!" appealed Kimpoc, turning to the bench. "I would stake my reputation that the accused is not an evildoer."

As Kimpoc returned to his seat, I flashed him an appreciative smile.

"Now, noble judges," Dundruhu completed his attack, "too much time has been spent on this case. I say no more, but leave the decision in your hands."

A long time went by. I saw the three judges huddled together on their damasked copper-red chairs. Out of nervousness, I stirred on my bench—and the sword of a Public Protector clanked warningly. Another long interval passed. Then the white-bearded one strode to the copper railing, and cleared his throat.

"My brothers and I agree," he droned, "that this case is flagrant, involving a deep-laid conspiracy to create dissension between us and our neighbors. The offense, moreover, is aggravated by the shameless way in which the accused has denied the charges. We would be justified in ordering transportation for life." He paused; the drone grew heavier; seemed to bore straight into me. "Nevertheless, we must not forget the word spoken on his behalf by one of our most respected citizens. My brothers and I have consequently agreed upon leniency."

He paused again, and a wild hope came to me.

"We refrain from ordering transportation for life," the voice droned on. "We condemn Munjin Alg to be sent to Project P or similar projects for twenty years of hard labor."

While one of the Public Protectors jerked me up from the bench, I saw the fat priest in his black tunic

110

once more waddling toward the judges' platform. And as I was dragged from the room, I heard again his solemn intonations, "Peace, honor, and right! Mercy, justice, and light!"

CHAPTER XVII

PROJECT J

Again the cold grip of steel; the cracking of whips; sharp streaks of pain along my shoulders; profane cries and bawling oaths in my ears. "Faster, you lazy dog! Faster!" Then a constant tugging as dozens of men tied to me in a long line, pulled at chains ahead of me, and dragged at chains behind.

Meanwhile I saw nothing at all, for black bands had been clamped over my eyes. Where we were going, I could not say, though the dusty winds told that we were in the open, and I knew we must be in some area of "Supreme Secrecy." We seemed to trudge an immense distance. But at last we began moving more slowly; stone pavements gave way to wooden; and we were prodded into a reeking interior.

After a time, I felt the fetters being snapped loose

from my wrists, and a rude hand pulled off my black eye-bands. At first, everything was still dark; then, in the unlighted gloom, I could make out a crowd of dim standing forms.

At about the same time we heard a sound as of motors, and the walls and floor began to shudder. Thuds, thumps, and bangings followed; with explosive jerks we lurched forward, and I had the feeling of being on a ship at sea as the walls and floor trembled and I felt a lunging, rolling, and plunging.

As my eyes adjusted themselves to the surroundings, I saw that we were in an oblong compartment about ten paces wide and half as long, where forty or fifty men were jammed together. The only ventilation was by means of two portholes, each about as large as a man's head; the men fought continually for a place near one of these openings. It was some time before I could work my way to either porthole—and then what a surprise! Above me the stars glittered, but no waves were shimmering just below. I seemed to look through an immense abyss to waters shining by the light of a half moon at a depth of thousands of feet.

"By the gods!" I groaned. "We're in a *thrittle!*"

A *thrittle* was a "flying boat" or "airboat," composed of a huge egg-shaped bag of gas, motors like those of giant *littos*, and a dangling passenger or cargo compartment. Considered unsafe for general travel, they were mostly used for freight.

"By Quabbu, what do you expect?" grumbled the man to my left. "What are we but just another kind of freight?"

I said nothing, but tried to digest the knowledge that we were being air-borne across the sea.

By the gray light of dawn, which after a time seeped in through the portholes, I began to recognize my traveling mates, who included most of those sen-

113

tenced at the trial. To my surprise, they looked at me almost with admiration.

"Brother, why didn't you tell us what you were after?" asked the one with the bloodshot eyes. "That plot of yours—to murder those Western swine as they came out of the *Prajn*—I'd have given my index finger to join you."

"Your plot was well enough thought out. But by Quabbu," spoke up the weedy youth with the slight twist in his face, "why make out you were innocent-white? That story about the love note was the flimsiest I ever heard."

No one seemed to hear my protest.

"Next time you make up any stories," the weedy youth went on, in friendly admonition, "remember our rule. Make your lies sound like truth. Otherwise, be strictly honest."

"I curse the gods that your dagger didn't drink blood!" snorted the prisoner with the bull-like face and bulging bull's eyes.

"But I didn't want to murder anyone!" I denied, almost in a shout. This, however, provoked only laughter. I saw that it would be useless to press my argument. Besides, I was feeling so miserable—so weak, so hungry, so nearly exhausted—that all I wanted was a spot large enough to sink down and soothe the savage aching in my head.

But before I could find such a haven, a shout rang out from a watcher at a porthole. "Land below!"

At the same time, amid a confusion of hoarse cries, the ship lurched downward, then lurched again, then slanted down at an angle of twenty or thirty degrees, while the cries became more and more excited.

"By Quabbu! we're almost there!" I heard a loud exclamation. There followed a jolt which threw us all abruptly forward; a door was thrown open and a voice bellowed at us, "Out, you ugly hounds! Out!"

114

Squirming, threshing, and pushing, we crowded through the doorway. Outside, the men huddled in a cringing mob, surrounded by sword-swinging guards in slate-gray tunics. I observed the *thrittle* looming above me, a huge rose-tinted, egg-shaped bag. To my right, rocky palisades towered, crowned by a squat, turreted, tiny-windowed stone building, and ringed with ramparts on which sentries paced. To my left, the blue sea splashed in whitecaps; near at hand, docks and wharves reached out, with small moored boats. And straight ahead of me there was a wide dusty field, where a company of soldiers, in red-striped gray tunics and with three-pointed glistening pikes, were marching round and round.

"This way, you wormy louts!" one of the guards yelled at us, swinging his sword and herding us away. Beneath an unclouded early morning sun, we wound past steel machines with wheels higher than houses; skirted vast mounds of rock and gravel; and passed hills whose sides had been sliced off like cake cut by a knife, leaving rock cliffs sheer as prison walls. Everywhere we saw men at work, loading the ships, piling bales and barrels on the piers, or driving clattering vehicles which looked like large rowboats, except that they ran on three wheels, one in front and two in the rear, and curved and twisted madly in all directions.

Half a dozen of the three-wheeled boatlike vehicles (which our masters called *chruggas*) came puffing up, and seven or eight of us were ordered into each machine, in addition to the driver and two guards.

Clinging to little backless benches, we were borne far across scarred landscapes, which were covered with enormous piles of rock and gravel; among the carved hills and leafless plains, everything was bare gray or brown.

"By all the gods! Where do they take us?" my

115

comrades kept muttering, as they struggled to hold to their shaking seats.

Suddenly the road dipped. I saw rock walls looming on both sides; these grew taller, until they rose far above. There came a roaring in my ears, a musty smell invaded my nostrils, and we dived into a tunnel, utterly black except for three copper-red lights on the prow of the car. But finally we saw light ahead. Then, as our speed began to slacken, we turned into a much larger tunnel, illuminated by amber light strips, and two or three times a man's height.

Here, in the close, hot air, all was fevered activity. We saw rows of rock-laden *chruggas* moving in a long line to the left, and empty *chruggas* in an equally long line to the right. We heard a commotion, as of multitudes of engines scraping, pounding, grinding, crunching, and drilling all at once; and saw the source of the commotion at the tunnel's end, where gigantic machines were swinging steel claws and steel jaws, ripping out great chunks of rock, and hurling them to the tunnel floor. There other machines, with iron hands, picked up the larger pieces and dumped them into waiting *chruggas*, while squads of men—naked except for loincloths—labored with spades and shovels to pile the smaller rock fragments into the vehicles. On one side, rows of blue steel kegs were marked "DANGER!"

Though the din was so great that not even a shout could be heard, we understood the gestures of the guards, who signalled us to take up spades and shovels. As I began wielding my tool, pitching bits of rock into the *chrugga*, an overseer with an unbared sword glared above me, and I knew that I had reached Project J.

CHAPTER XVIII

STORM WARNINGS

The room was dark, stone-walled, and brick-floored, and no longer than you could cross in four strides. Along each side wall and the front one, three narrow straw-filled triple bunks had been built, one above the other, and the front wall had just room also for a narrow iron-barred door. To the rear, a partition could be pulled in and out; when it was withdrawn, only an iron railing remained, and beyond the railing a long drop to the waves that foamed against jumbled rocks. The room had no furniture other than the nine bunks and one dirty old straw mattress on the floor.

My nine fellow prisoners, I learned, were all *suantitts* or "super-offenders"; among them were pirates, arsonists, kidnappers, and murderers. And yet they received me as one of their own. "By the horns of a goat! we've heard all about you!" I was greeted by a grizzled old fellow named Yimbac. "So you're the lion who wanted to do away with those snakes from the Western Isles!"

In a morose silence, I ranged about the room and stood by the iron railing in the gathering twilight, staring out at the breakers lashing the rocks far below.

"Nobody yet ever got away from this worm-eaten island of Zug," the grizzled prisoner asserted, as if reading my mind. "Blast the idea out of your head, mate. Only two have ever tried it. Ah, well, nobody can say what happened to them."

But if I had no chance of escape for twenty long, hard years, I might as well leap over the iron railing to the jagged rocks. Only one thing deterred me: the thought of Lampra, the remembrance of her tear-filled dark eyes, and the hope—which stubbornly persisted—that sometime we would be reunited.

Day by day, as I watched the tunnelling operations, I never ceased to wonder about their meaning. On the second day, to my relief, I was given a new job: to drive one of the machines, or *chruggas*, which was run very simply by means of a guiding stick and buttons. My task now was to wait in the tunnel until other laborers had filled the *chrugga*, then drive it out, slide the car's bottom off by pulling a lever, and pour the contents upon one of the mounds of waste. Then I would replace the bottom, drive the *chrugga* back into the tunnel, and repeat the loading and unloading.

All the while, a dread suspicion was fastening itself upon me. Why should the island of Zug be the center of all this activity? This question I asked everyone, including the guards and my fellow prisoners, but the usual reply was a shrug. Then one day a guard snarled at me warningly, "Don't you know this is a

118

Supreme Secrecy project? Better put a clasp over those reckless lips of yours!"

I did indeed put a clasp over my lips, but could not seal up my mind. I knew that the immense and costly tunnel under the sea was not being drilled for the sake of better transportation to so unimportant a place as Zug. So what was its purpose? My thoughts wandered back to a day, now seeming infinitely far off, when Wauglan Waud addressed the *Kolem*. His very words, which had often come back to me in nightmares, repeated themselves in my mind, "All we have to do is bore a secret tunnel under the sea . . . turn the tunnel into an overheated boiler without escape valve."

This, then, explained the excavations. The tunnel from Zug was an experimental bore, like the one proposed by Waud for the Cocoanut Islands. It was meant to test the feasibility of war by volcanic eruption! Waud's plans had been reported by spies to the high command of the Eastern Isles; and, consequently, the Eastern Isles and the Western were engaged in a race to mutual destruction.

As this terrible realization swept over me, my own problems appeared petty, unimportant. What did matter was that Atlantis was endangered. If I could only get word to the Western Isles that their plans were being copied in the East, then perhaps the mad competition would be checked before too late.

But could I report my discovery in time? As the first step, I must win my freedom; and this seemed impossible as I stared out at the wide waters, gazed up at the pikes and swords of innumerable guards, and saw myself everywhere followed by suspicious eyes.

But it is something to have a hope to sustain one. There was, however, little else to uphold me. As time went by, I was being worn and aged. My long, ragged

119

hair and beard were becoming grizzled at the edges. My tall, slender frame took on a new gauntness; there were hollows in my cheeks and beneath my eyes.

Three years went by. And then I witnessed an event that told me how terribly justified I had been in opposing Waud and his kind.

During these years, work had never ceased on the tunnel, which had been aimed toward Clento Island, far to the south. But as the excavations proceeded, progress became slower, because of the growing difficulties of cooling and ventilation and the longer haul. Toward the end, I could make but one or two round trips a day on my *chrugga*. At about this time, excited rumors began to fill the air: Project J was approaching its end—changes lay in store for us all.

Changes certainly did lie in store on one grim day when we were ordered not to work as usual, but remained locked in our cells. I passed my time gazing moodily out across the heaving blue waters, where a few small red, purple, or chrome-yellow sails flapped in the breeze. Far to the south, I could see the azure cloudy masses which I now knew to be the island of Clento, described by my cellmates as a forested green paradise.

My reflections were interrupted by a jolt, as if some gigantic jaw had taken hold of our prison, and shaken it. I had felt earthquakes before, and not a few right here on Zug, but never one so violent as this, which lasted for the time of a hundred heartbeats, while rumblings came from the earth around us, and great rocks cannonaded down the cliffs.

Terrified, we all threw ourselves to the floor. The stone ceiling was bulging downward; the bars of the cell door were bent.

"Curse those fiends of the under-caves!" growled Yimbak. "I thought they were going to bury us alive!"

120

"What a coincidence," I muttered, "the one day we're locked up—"

"You're crazier, mate, than a stag at rutting time if you think it's a coincidence!" interrupted Yimbak. "Those hyenas of keepers knew very well why they locked us up!"

A succession of minor earthquakes followed. And then one of the men, pointing to sea, let out a cry. "Great Quabbu! See that smoke!"

Far to the south, toward Clento Island, we could make out a cloud rising above land—a peculiar cloud, rapidly expanding in the shape of a funnel, which gave place to that of an enormous tree, with a thick dark trunk, and wide umbrellalike limbs.

"The gods help us now!" I wailed. "The Clento volcanoes are erupting!"

"The sea! The sea! Look at the sea!" one of the men yelled.

Horrified, we watched as a foamy line moved toward us from the far distance with the speed of a swallow flying. As it drew nearer, it gathered force and size; gulls and other sea birds began wheeling out of view with weird screams and screeches; and small red, purple, and yellow sails were overtaken and washed under. But still the water swept on, a rolling, foaming white wall, which burst against the rocks beneath us with a roar as of all the cataracts on earth. And our lips knew the taste of salt.

Then, with equal fury, the wave retreated, and great stretches of sand and shoals were drained dry. But we knew that it would soon come lashing back.

Meanwhile we still stood staring out at that portentous southern sky, in which the treelike spread of smoke was widening and darkening, almost from the eastern horizon to the western. As night approached, lightning began to flicker and fork; and after the sun had set in a sea of blood-red, the smoke cloud was lighted with deepening crimson, varied by vermilion and orange-yellow, while the rattling of thunder was in the air, and the floor beneath us continued to tremble. Not long after sunset, tormenting odors came to our nostrils, the suffocating reek of sulphur; and a gusty wind was thick with cinders. At the same time, an oppressive heat had settled over us.

"The gods help us now! It's the world's end!" one of the men foretold.

Just then, from the skies above Clento Island, there came the most startling demonstration of all. The glowing cloud was split by a sword of white light. Blades of white, and of eerie green and blue, began shooting in all directions; the whole prodigious crimson cloud puffed upward. In a few seconds it had filled the sky, which had taken fire with a red furnace-fury; incandescent patches of sunlight brilliance blazed from the direction of the island. Simultaneously, we were almost withered by a wave of heat; and the floor began to heave like a foundering ship.

By the palpitating light of the heavens, I could see the ceiling bulging downward more dangerously; could see, also, a zigzag crack in the floor. And I noticed that the smoke above Clento extended much further than before—a trunk of red flame as wide as the island itself.

"It's the world's end! World's end!" several men repeated the cry. Others, reverting to old superstitions, were down on their knees, muttering prayers.

"What can it be? What can it be?" the men kept asking, when the booming and thundering was interrupted long enough to permit them to be heard. But I already knew. With each breaker that slapped in foam against the cliffs, the words of the Seeress of the Dawn once more crashed back to my mind. "Small storms precede great! Small storms precede great! Small storms precede great!"

Then, after the long night had dragged away and the sultry mists in the direction of Clento Island gradually disappeared, I received another shock. In the sunlight that shone clear and strong again across the southern waves, I looked in vain for the familiar cloudy azure masses my eyes had rested upon so often. Where Clento Island should have been, the ocean stretched unbroken.

CHAPTER XIX

THE CAPTAIN OF THE GUARDS

"Those blazing incompetents of generals did more than they expected," Yimbak surmised, as we stood gazing at the open waste. "Why should they want to wipe out the whole island?"

"Why should they care what they wipe out?" I argued, trying to collect my thoughts. For it had come to me that I had been watching much more than the destruction of one small island. If only the Western leaders could be made to realize how far the Eastern Isles had advanced in volcanic warfare, then surely Waud and his kind would understand the need of halting the plunge toward ruin!

"At least," I said, "Project J is over. Maybe now our masters won't work us so hard."

"Maybe not—but I never yet knew a rat to change its hide," argued Yimbak.

Next morning, sure enough, we began work on project K. And this, from all that I could make out, was a repetition of Project J, except that the new tunnel was being built toward Wertyu Island, to our east. At first the only evident change was in the new set of guards, which caused most of us to mutter in dread. True, we had unanimously hated the old guards, but their successors were even more brutal; soon we all bore their crimson whip marks. Yet one of them did turn out to be different.

His name was Yutir, and he kept much to himself, not fraternizing with the other guards, who seemed in awe of him, as well they might be, since he was their captain. He was an imposingly tall, broad-shouldered man, with a sharp, strong face, a slightly twisted eagle's beak of a nose above a wide brush of a mustache, and a large crescent-shaped scar on his left cheek. His eyes were a deep burning blue, which in some lights turned to purple or to a sullen black.

Like the other prisoners, I was intimidated by Yutir, though his lash never crackled down on our shoulders. But that I should ever get to know him—that we should become friendly—this would have seemed as likely as for the hunted stag to associate with the hounds.

Our contact started with one of those accidents that were not uncommon in our operations. One day I had just brought my *chrugga* into the excavation, which was filled as usual with the din of digging machines, when the commotion ceased, giving way to an agonized scream; Yimbak, as he worked at the excavator, had got one leg caught in the crunching metal teeth. Writhing, he lay on the floor, a red stream pouring from his injured limb.

Many another such mishap I had seen; I knew that

125

the first necessity was to stop the flow of blood. I leapt off the *chrugga*, and started toward the victim. But a guard named Arbac shouldered himself into our path.

"Let the toad be!" he snarled. "Get back to your work!"

With a swinging lash, he blocked the way to the fallen man. But while I stood hesitating, an immense figure sprang in front of me, towering a foot above the other guard.

"Quabbu help us!" Yutir's voice boomed forth. "This man must be saved! Come, men, where are your hands?"

Along with Yutir and one or two others, I dashed past the glowering Arbac; then tore off a strip of my tunic, made a tourniquet of it, and began to stanch the bleeding.

As I worked, Yutir remained to help until the flow of blood had been checked. Then, turning to me, he rumbled, "This man must be taken where he can rest and recuperate. Here! What about a shoulder lift?"

Three of us immediately lifted Yimbak to our shoulders and, following Yutir's directions, bore him to a little room cut in the rock walls near the tunnel entrance. From the sight of a guard's slate-gray spare uniform dangling from a hook, we knew that this room was for Yutir's private use; and we were surprised when he cautioned, "Gently, there!", and ordered us to put the patient on the straw cot in a corner. "After a time, he can go back to his cell," he diagnosed. "He'll be as strong again as ever."

Turning to me, he directed, "Stay here with the sufferer till the working day is over. Be with you later!"

But soon Yimbak was delirious. His wound had to be bound again, and he had to be given water. Hours went by; finally, to my relief, he slept. And while he was sleeping, Yutir returned.

Our eyes, as the guard bent inquiringly over the sleeping man, chanced to meet; and I saw the sympathy in their blue depths. "Let him sleep!" Yutir said, with an abruptness that did not deceive me. "When he wakes, we'll get him to that room over there!"

He jerked a finger toward a door to the right. "Meanwhile, stay here!" And then, with a yawn, "By Quabbu! I'm more tired than an old hound, but still have work to do."

He swung his spare uniform back from its hook on the wall, bringing to view a small dresser from which he took a sheaf of papers and a writing stick. At the same time, he stepped on a floor switch, and a whole wall glowed bright yellow. With a mumbled oath, he seated himself cross-legged on the floor, while I watched him pore over the papers.

For many minutes he glowered at them, then, with a growl, he flung them from him. "Claws of a sand crab!" he grumbled, more to himself than to me. "After a man's grubbed all day like a mole in the ground, it's an insult to expect him to waste time on computations!"

"Computations? What kind of computations?"

With one hand, he jerked savagely at the faintly grizzled red-brown of his mustache. Something inchoate came out of his throat.

"You know," I went on, hastily, "computations are one of my specialties. At Admenebda, I worked as a computator."

"Oh! By Quabbu! you must enjoy punishment!"

"To me, working with figures was always a sort of game."

"A devil's game!" he rasped. And pointing to the writing stick and papers, "Three nights I've slaved over that donkey report, and still can't get it straight!"

"Maybe I can help," I dared to suggest. "That is, if it's nothing secret."

Yutir, with a sharp thrust of his slightly twisted eagle's beak of a nose, swung back toward me. "That's a pleasure I wouldn't deny anyone," he acquiesced, wrily.

But as I began poring over the sheets, I found nothing really difficult. There were columns of figures to add, subtract, and multiply, and percentages to compute concerning man-days of labor at Project K. It was all simple enough; almost no time had passed before I had tabulated all the columns.

"Great Quabbu! How do you do it?" marvelled Yutir. "Sure this is all correct?"

I went over the figures again, but found no error.

"You *are* a wizard!" he applauded, gratitude in his eyes. "When some new devils' reports come in to be filled out, maybe you'll let me have some more of your magic?"

"Such as it is," I agreed. And just then Yimbak turned on one side with a groan, opened his eyes, and asked for water. Yutir now decided that, between us, we could remove him to the other room, a dim, straw-filled hole with just space enough for the patient to lie down in.

"We'll have to keep him here two or three days," Yutir foretold. "Meanwhile, you stay with him, Munjin Alg," Yutir went on. "By Quabbu! it won't ruin Project K to have one worker less for a few days!"

"What of my cell mates? They'll wonder that I don't return—won't they think I'm getting special privileges?"

"Yes, by my hide! they *will* think so!" Yutir roared. "Special privileges for breaking the rules—down in the Black Pit!"

I joined in the laughter. And thus a bond was sealed between me and the captain of the guards.

CHAPTER XX

DESPERATE PLANS

For the third or fourth time, I squatted opposite Yutir in his small underground room, poring over figures. "I think you'll find these correct," I said, passing him several papers; then reluctantly arose, for the idea of returning to my cell had no charms for me.

"Sit down!" Yutir ordered, peremptorily. "By Quabbu, Munjin Alg, you owe me an explanation."

By the brilliant yellow of the illuminated wall, I noticed that he was staring at me searchingly.

"In my day, Munjin," he rumbled on, "I've met every kind of man. But never another like you. When I look up the records, I find you're held for conspiracy against the State, and attempted assassination. That, by Quabbu! is hard to understand."

"It shouldn't be hard," I answered, surprised that he

should be interested in me. "I know you won't believe it, but I was arrested on false charges. A love note I had written was mistaken for a letter of treason."

"By my hide! how so?"

I related the details, but withheld Lampra's name and identity. And Yutir's eyes narrowed with a concentration of interest.

"The gods bear witness, it's a good story!" he testified, when I had finished. "I too, Munjin, have known the sting of false accusations."

"You?" I asked. "But you're not a prisoner."

"A guard may also be a prisoner!" he snapped. He rose to his full gigantic height, and slashed at the air. "Do you think I'd come of my own free will to a devils' hole like this, to be buried underground and never see any human being but those scamps of prisoners and even worse scamps of guards?"

Astonished, I said nothing. But Yutir, after a savage stride or two about the room, went on. "I too was sent here as a punishment. By Quabbul just to be here is a cruel chastisement!"

"That I know."

"Where do you think I was before?" he rushed on, with an aggressive thrust of his eagle's beak of a nose. "At Buztubra! It's on an island, smaller than this vile Zug, separated by a narrow channel from the big city of Anchartu. Because the channel's so narrow, and has no sharks, little boats must patrol constantly, to see that no prisoner escapes. I was in charge of one boat."

Yutir's face lit up; a reminiscent pleasure put a glow into the rough, trenched features. "Ah, that was a man's life! All day in the wind and sun, with the good salt spray splashing in your face, and the salty tang in your nostrils. Even in stormy weather, I went to work as to an adventure."

"Still, you had to catch prisoners, if they tried to escape—"

130

"*If* they tried to. But they never did. That is—" He hesitated, and thunder clouded his brow. "That is, except once."

As he majestically stalked about the room, his head almost touched the ceiling. "There were three brother guards of mine. One was a terrier-faced runt named Quizzu, who was jealous because I was a captain and he was only a common guard. He was the weaver of the scheme."

"So there was a plot against you?"

"Yes! Once every tenth day, I had a day off, like all the guards; and usually went to Anchartu, where the gold-haired girls are the most pleasing in all Atlantis. I had one there that—but, oh, well—"

He halted; spat out disgustedly; and rushed on. "One day, while I was in Anchartu, three prisoners escaped, after which that yellow rat Quizzu led the investigators to my boat *Flying Spray*. There they found several articles hidden—a ring, a punctured coin, and some other trash of the escaped men. Quizzu charged they'd escaped in my boat, with my help. This shouldn't have deceived a half-witted sheep— Quizzu had plainly planted the supposed evidence."

"Wasn't that easy to prove?"

"How was I to prove it? No one saw Quizzu put the articles there, and the red-faced liar swore he was on a job at the far end of the island. So he was! But it would have been simple enough to sneak in at night. Naturally, I defended myself, but there's nothing so hard as to make another man see inside your heart. I was found guilty by the *Bunto*, the Court of Prison Directors. But as this was my first offense, I wasn't thrown out of the service—just sent to the worst place in the system for five years—*five years!*"

Yutir turned from me with a groan.

"Sometimes I wonder if I can stand it," he went on, glumly. "I see the green waves splashing, and feel the

131

white spray on my cheeks, and I'd turn the world upside down to get back to my boat!"

With a whirlwind change of manner, he wheeled upon me. "Why do I tell you all this? By Quabbu! We've wasted too much time. Now get back to your cell!".

The barriers between us, however, had been broken down. Many another time he invited me to his room, even when the computations were a transparent pretext. The man, I saw, was as lonely as I; his taciturnity before the other guards was only a mask. But with me he spoke more freely as he told of his past, his birthplace on the small sea island of Iru, and his drifting into work as a guard when he came to Anchartu looking for employment and was recommended because of his imposing physique. I, in turn, told him of my life in Admenebda, though I never mentioned the Western Isles.

Often I would find him in a grim, angry mood. "It's enough, Munjin, to make the gods hold their noses, the way Project K is run," he would grumble. "It's a spiderweb, and you and I have our legs caught tight in it."

The climax came after half a year. One day he asked me to step in to see him after work; but when I arrived, I found him lying on a heap of straw, panting, and with nothing but a loincloth to cover his hairy red skin.

"That pig of a *Tuy!*" he muttered; and mouthed a bitter oath. "He has to pick just today for his meannesses—hottest day the gods have punished us with for years!"

"What meannesses?"

Yutir let out a string of curses. But finally I made out that a large new batch of prisoners would be placed under his charge next day, adding greatly to his labors. "By Quabbu, just think of it! I'll have to

132

make records and computations for every one of that filthy gang!"

"I'll help with the computations."

He turned aside as if he did not hear.

"If I could only fly off like a sea gull," he mumbled, "then, by all the devils, they wouldn't find me here another minute!"

"I've often wondered why you can't just quit your job."

"If I could quit, would I be here now?" he barked. "No, like a headless hen, I signed up originally for ten years, and have nearly five more to drag out. If I ran away and was caught, I'd be back again, but not in a guard's uniform. Just the same, I've about made up my mind to risk it."

His voice became lower, more secretive; he glanced warily up and down.

"Anywhere in the Eastern Isles, I'd be a hunted man. Only chance is in foreign parts, like the Western Isles. However, I have no prejudices—the Western Islanders are human too."

"I don't mind telling you a secret, Yutir. I myself am from the Western Isles."

"By Quabbu, you don't say so? Well, I always did wonder about your queer way of talking. But that doesn't matter. Now listen carefully, Munjin!"

Again he glanced about him furtively. "I've figured things all out. There is a way to escape. One man couldn't do it. But two might. Do you think, Munjin," he asked, plaintively, "you could—"

"I'd risk a den of tigers to get out."

"Just how I feel!" he concurred, and brought his big fist down with a thump. "What if I do lose my neck? It's not worth a puff of wind to me here. Still, Munjin, you understand the risk—"

I did indeed understand. But in order to escape, I would have jumped into a live volcano.

"Yes, I've figured things out," Yutir repeated, his deep-blue eyes glistening. "You know how many small supply boats dock at the island. The guards have to bring things to and from the boats. Well then, what's to stop me from getting into one of them—one all laden with provisions—and putting out to sea?"

"But can you do that all by yourself?"

He shook his head emphatically.

"No! The Western Isles—by the stars, that's a ten or fifteen days' cruise. One man would have to manage the boat while one slept."

My heart sank. "Managing a boat—that's something quite outside my experience."

"It won't be outside your experience—not after our first night! I'll teach you all you need to know. . . . And so, Munjin my friend—what do you say?"

He stared at me so beseechingly that I could hardly have refused even if I had not been all afire to accept.

"The first dark, cloudy night, Munjin. I'll give you the signal," he promised. And then, with a sigh, he turned over on one side—and our interview was over.

CHAPTER XXI

HO FOR THE WESTERN ISLES!

"You've missed your place in life, Munjin. You should have been a guard!" Yutir exclaimed, his blue eyes bright with laughter, though he kept his voice under control.

I faced him a little doubtfully, draped in his over-large spare slate-gray guard's uniform.

With a pair of shears, he skillfully applied himself to my full beard, and when he had finished, it was no longer ragged. "By Quabbu! I've had practice," he explained. "We guards always play barber to each other. If no one stares too closely, you'll pass."

He picked up a minute spherical electric torch, and secreted it in the folds of his garment. "Well, shall we go?"

All the furtiveness of the hunting animal came

135

upon him. His eyes grew narrow and opaque. He opened his door by a hand's breadth, and warily glanced out. "Ready?"

I grunted something that sounded like "Yes."

"If we meet anyone, just go along as if we'd not a thing under heaven to fear," he cautioned. "Keep at my side, do as I do—but don't talk unless you have to."

Speechlessly, we glided into the corridor, a small pedestrian passageway, which led us into the open night.

We paused to take exhilarating breaths of the clean, fresh air. The sky was morosely dark, with low-banked clouds that threatened rain. There was a long row of poles just before us, each bearing dim, down-turning amber light strips, which barely showed us the narrow foot path. Some distance ahead of us, there was a somewhat brighter glow in the direction of the docks.

Skulking like ghosts, we made our way with heads bent low. The phosphorescent green eyes of a hunting cat stared at us out of the gloom. Then, as we drew near the water, two men lunged into sight with lanterns swinging. I thought that I could make out the slate gray of guards' uniforms.

The lanterns swept forward; flashed into our eyes. But Yutir calmly flung one hand up in salute. "Bad night, brothers, to be out in!" he boomed, forcing a laugh.

"A night that's accursed of the gods, brothers!" heartily replied one of the strangers.

As we approached the docks, my companion swung about in a wide circle, avoiding the illuminated areas. Keeping to a fringe of blackness, most of the time with sheds or fences between us and the water, we felt our way amid dense shadows.

At last we had reached a dark, deserted section of

the waterfront. Hearing the waves lapping against the piers, I moved snail-like after Yutir. Then I felt small splashes in my hands as the rain began, swiftly increasing to a torrent. "The gods have sent us luck!" Yutir decided, putting his lips close to my ear. "In such a night, no one will be abroad."

Emboldened, he flashed on the electric torch, which let out a very faint light. With its aid, we could just make out the dark hulks of moored small boats, all of them unlighted, and evidently unoccupied; Yutir leapt to the deck of one as it creaked complainingly in the storm.

"No good, by Quabbu!" he reported, after climbing down a hatch. "It's emptier than an old clam shell!"

Painfully he repeated the experiment with four other small ships, but all had discharged their cargo.

"We'll take a chance, even without provisions!" he at last resolved. "But have the gods no pity? Look!"

As suddenly as it had begun, the rain squall ended; a half-moon was shining through a slit in the clouds.

Nevertheless, this light may have saved us, for it showed us several casks standing in front of a partly loaded ship. Agilely Yutir sprinted to the vessel's deck; his great muscles flexing and unflexing, he tugged to free the mooring ropes as I came panting up. Then, with a savage wrench, he released the cables.

As the craft drifted free, he dived into the small, dark cabin, torch in hand; his practiced fingers, working at the instrument panel, soon caused a steady hum to sound from somewhere in the vessel's heart. He slowly maneuvered the small ship into the channel between the piers.

But, a moment later, I thought that our haste had betrayed us, for we saw orange-red lanterns approaching along the shore like searching eyes rapidly converging toward us, amid yells and shouts.

"Quabbu help us now!" Yutir muttered. But his

fingers worked more furiously than ever, and gradually we gained speed. Recklessly, as the lanterns drew together near the pier, we shot south toward the open waters.

At that moment, to our great relief, the moon hid her head again among the clouds; the sound of sudden heavy rain was once more in our ears. And while the splashing fury of the shower drowned out the thud-thud of the motors, we headed more swiftly into the heaving wilderness of black.

Then, as Yutir sweated to press every ounce of power out of the engines and the frail craft pitched and rolled, the downpour ceased as suddenly as it had begun; as if a veil had lifted, we saw several diverging ruby-red lights bobbing toward us from the direction of the island.

"The gods preserve us!" Yutir muttered. "They'll be on all sides of us before you can wink twice!"

He turned a switch, pulled a lever; we swung about so abruptly that a wave nearly engulfed us. Then, with our eyes still on those bobbing ruby-red lights, we swerved at right angles. An anxious moment passed, while the red lights plunged ahead just as before. But even as we congratulated each other, long golden searchlights began sweeping the sea, and two of the red lights streaked toward us.

"More speed! More speed!" I commanded, desperately.

Yutir cursed beneath his breath. The two ruby-red lights still swept toward us. Just then our ears caught a sound as of waves breaking, and the moon let down light enough to show a huge jagged dark mass towering alarmingly near.

"By Quabbu! We nearly smashed into it!" cried Yutir, recognizing one of the tiny uninhabited off-shore islands.

He turned again, at an angle of about fifty degrees;

but just as we began passing around the island, he headed our craft with a ferocious jerk straight toward the shore. Terrified visions came to me of a crash. But no! we slid into a small cove where, with mountainous cliffs looming black on both sides, we cast anchor just as the moon dived back behind the clouds. Hardly a minute later, two ruby-red lights glided past.

Hours went by. The red lights returned, moving slowly and doubtfully; the golden searchlight beams swung up and down but could not spy us out.

When the first gray of dawn gave us light enough to maneuver by, Yutir steered the craft deeper into the cove, while I pulled down a long red-and-yellow banner identifying the ship as the *Storm Strider*.

"If necessary, we'll stay here for days," Yutir decided. "At last, thanks to the gods, we're free!" he exulted. "Free, free to live a man's life!"

"Free! Free! Free!" I chimed in, joining Yutir in a dance of delight. But all at once I halted. Far to the east, barely visible above the rim of the cliff, an egg-shaped, rose-tinted mass was drifting in the air.

Yutir too saw it; and threw himself flat beside me on the deck. "A *thrittle*! Won't those fiends ever give up the hunt?"

For a long while we lay on deck, while the great egg-shaped bag glided out of sight and returned, hovering uncertainly.

"Remember, we're a very small object, down here beside these tall cliffs," Yutir pointed out. "Even if they do see us, how will they know who we are?"

Finally, after the *thrittle* had remained out of view much longer than usual, he dared to rise; pointed to the foamy green waters; and muttered a vow. "I swear by my honor those beasts will never take me alive!"

"I swear the same!" I pledged, as I arose.

He put one hand on my shoulder and we stood

there in a resolute silence—two grim, determined men who understood one another.

But, a minute later, we had plunged back into action; stripped off our guards' uniforms; wrapped them in heavy rocks; and pitched them into the water. "Two clues gone!" Yutir grunted, with satisfaction; then darted below, and emerged in a few minutes with a pair of sea-green sailors' tunics.

Now, for the first time, we had a chance to examine the *Storm Strider*. She was of about five times a man's length, and had but one deck, a small cabin barely large enough to accommodate the two of us, a hold containing the motors and cargo compartments, and a mast with a sail for use in emergencies.

"We're going to need that sail," Yutir reported, glumly. "There's only fuel for a day or two. But worse, cursed be the gods, there's not food or water enough, either! Well, by Quabbu! we can get along for a few days by skimping."

"Just the same, we'll make it!" I predicted.

"So, by the gods, we will! We'll hide here another day or two, and then ho for the Western Isles!"

"Ho for the Western Isles!" I echoed.

As we waited, thick clouds gathered, and the thought came to me that, both in the Eastern Isles and the Western, I was now a hunted man, sought by the authorities and in peril of my life.

CHAPTER XXII

THE ORDEAL OF THE STORM STRIDER

A foggy drizzle blanketed the sea beneath a stagnant gray overcast; the waves, whitely lashing the rocks, made a crashing monotone that drowned out the churring of our engines as we slowly made our way out of the cove. For three days we had awaited just such a morning, while we had augmented our scanty rations by scrambling about among the rocks of the islet, greedily helping ourselves to clams and other shellfish, and robbing birds' nests.

Far in the distance, as we picked our way forward, we heard the hollow roar of fog sirens, and we knew that other ships were abroad. After a time, when we were well out of the cove, Yutir began steering our ship forward with reckless speed.

A little later, the sun burst through the mist, and

we saw the unending tossing blue sea, while behind us a long line of fog veiled the land from sight.

"The gods have blessed us, Munjin!" Yutir cried, clapping me on the shoulder, while his blue eyes took flame and he steered with one hand. "Now I'll teach you seamanship!"

This he proceeded to do very thoroughly. I learned to tend the motors, to steer, to judge direction by a little instrument with a magnetic pointer, to compute distance by dead reckoning, to reef and furl the sail, to tack in the wind, and to cast anchor. Soon, thanks to his expert instruction, I was able to take over many duties.

One duty was to tend the net which he had fashioned out of a surplus section of the sail. Dangling behind us in the water, while I guided it and pulled it in whenever necessary, the net brought us some small fry, which we gobbled raw. At the same time, a strip of sailcloth, stretched in the prow in the shape of a basin, gathered occasional rainwater.

Day after day went by—six days, eight, ten. Still we went bobbing on our way, avoiding distant large islands and great egg-shaped passing vessels. In four or five days more, we reckoned, we should reach the Western Isles. But to what port should we head? When I suggested Kallendra, Yutir immediately agreed. "One city or another—it matters little to me," he assented.

But a fierce unrest clutched me at the thought that I should so soon be back in my native city. In Kallendra, surely, I would see Lampra again! Also, I would greet my friend Langhis—Langhis, whom I had been unable to communicate with for fear of message tappers. In Kallendra, again, I might deliver my information as to Eastern volcanic experiments, and might yet help to save Atlantis.

But soon I began wondering whether we should

ever reach Kallendra. For twelve days, we had been favored by those mysterious beings, the gods of the weather; on the thirteenth day, a change came. An oppression hung in the air; the sky gradually thickened, as if veils of moisture had accumulated from nowhere, dimming and finally blanketing out the light of the sun. Then, low against the southern horizon, a purple cloud patch began to form. And the waves became choppy and agitated.

"By Quabbu!" cried Yutir. "It will be a real blow!" And motioning me to the steering rod, he began to pull in the sail with quick, excited movements, until the cloth was tightly furled about the mast. Then he carefully examined the hatches, making sure they all were secure.

My depression deepened as I felt the first wind against my cheek and the rain splashed down. And when, sometime later, the purple cloud patch included all the heavens and distant lightning began to fork and flash through the deep afternoon twilight, a grim, set look possessed Yutir's beaked face.

Gradually the gale developed, and never had I seen, never imagined such a shrieking, howling fury. All around us it was almost black. The wind seemed to come from all directions at once; it cuffed us, it buffeted us, it lashed and smashed and pounded us, and at times lifted us twiglike among the waves. Now we would seem about to be inundated; now we would be flying over the peak of a vast billow, then slanting down into another raging valley, then submerged amid a cascading commotion.

All the while, the din was terrifying, as if all the fiends of hell had joined in one, with a constant crashing, hammering and banging as loose objects slid about. When in time twilight had yielded to the blackness of night, our only illumination was from the lightning that hurled its knives of fire above. A

143

hundred times, I felt that the next blow would be the last. And yet somehow, after each wrenching and bludgeoning, we righted ourselves and pitched and staggered on our way.

All the nights I had ever endured before heaped into one, seemed to hold fewer hours than that long-drawn-out horror. Yet finally, after eons and epochs, there did come a faint brightening above. But the heavens were filled with a ragged scud of slaty clouds, and the waves still tossed tumultuously.

"Thanks to the gods, it's not so bad now," proclaimed Yutir. But I noticed how haggard he was, how dishevelled his hair, how bloodshot his eyes, and how there was a crimson mark above his left eye.

Then I saw how my tunic was torn off, and was aware for the first time of the bruises on my shins and chest, and the gash on my forehead.

Gradually, we were able to appraise our situation. We groaned to see all things inside the cabin tumbled together in confusion, and most of the instruments broken. With a curse, Yutir pointed through the heavy plastic cabin porthole. Half the rail was gone! The deck was twisted as by hammer blows! And where the mast had been, there was only a snapped-off pole.

"But the motors?" I gasped. "What about the motors?"

"We've used our last fuel!"

As the two of us stood, clutching at the walls of that wrecked and rocking cabin, we felt no further need for speech. Adrift in mid-sea with neither sails nor usable motors, we were in a plight that defied words. Worst of all, our fishnet had been washed overboard and our tumblers of water broken.

Much later, when the storm had died down sufficiently to permit us on deck, we set to work. Making use of the remaining scrap of sail and the stub of a mast, we contrived a distress signal—all we could do, except to keep a constant lookout, and to pray.

"I still say the sea gods will never desert us," Yutir foresaw, regaining his optimism as we stood clinging to the remaining half of the rail. "Sooner or later, some ship will come this way!"

But we saw no ship that day; and when another night had gone by, we began to feel delirious from hunger, but even more miserable from thirst.

For unending hours we still watched and waited while nothing happened, nothing at all to break the monotony of our gruelling, heartbreaking drifting. But toward the third day's close, Yutir cried out, and began pointing as a cloudy gray mass approached from the east.

The vessel seemed likely to pass us to starboard as we stood on deck, waving wildly, and shouting as loudly as our cracked throats permitted. But as the stranger drew nearer, her now retractable lookout tower projecting from the highest point of her otherwise almost featureless granite-hued egg-shaped hull, I received a fresh shock. The newcomer looked exactly like the *Swordfish!*

Almost I wished she would pass on. But as her approaching hulk began to loom large, Yutir let out a sobbing gasp. "She's slowing down!" At first, I thought that he was delirious. But soon I saw that the great vessel's speed really was slackening.

Finally, several stones' throws to starboard, she had almost halted. Watching in fevered impatience, we saw a hatch open in her side, while something long and tube-shaped slid out. And as this object splashed into the water, we saw three bobbing shapes inside it.

In a few minutes, the small boat had rowed near enough for us to make out its occupants. They were waving excitedly; within a boat's length of us, they came almost to a halt; and a red-bearded giant shouted in the distinctive accent of the Western Isles, "Who are you, mates? Where do you hail from?"

"Who are you? What is your ship?"

"The good vessel *Green Turtle*, of Kallendra!"

What a relief to know she was not the *Swordfish* after all!

"We too are from Kallendra!" I yelled back, remembering the story I had thought out long in advance. "We were on a fishing cruise. The storm gods caught us!"

"The storm gods nearly caught *us*!" called back the red-beard. "By Ablum! What a blow! Come! Our orders are to take you off that leaky old log!" A little unsteadily, we climbed over the rail into the *Green Turtle*. Then, after long, deep draughts of water, we were led up several flights to a cabin where a stern-looking man with a brushy brown beard was awaiting us. "Captain Orfgu! By the grace of the gods, here they are!" the red-beard introduced us.

Orfgu looked at us steadily, and at first said nothing. But there was a twinkle in his live brown eyes as, in response to his questions, I gave my name as Munjin Alg and repeated my story of the fishing cruise and the storm.

"Teeth of a shark!" he swore. "Great Ablum must want you to live, or he would not have saved you in such a gale!"

"All that we ask," I pleaded, "is to get back to Kallendra. We've lost everything in the storm. We'll work for our passage. Will we not, Yutir?"

"By the stars! we'll be grateful!"

"As the gods would have it," Orfgu informed us, while he leaned back against the steel knobs and green plastic dials of a long instrument panel, "we are outbound to the island of Ajaka, then to Zuttel in the Cocoanut Isles, then back to the Western Isles. Kallendra will be our last stop."

146

My heart sank at the thought of many another long weary day before we could reach Kallendra.

But Yutir's voice rang out gaily.

"Always I said the sea gods would save us. What matter how long it takes to reach Kallendra? May the gods, Captain Orfgu, bring long life to you and all your kin!"

Then, while the ship gave a series of convulsive shudders and started again, I heard Orfgu calling out to a seaman to give us food, clothing, and a place to rest.

CHAPTER XXIII

HOME PORT

For days I lay in a fever, often delirious. Sometimes, in dreams, I would hear Lampra calling and would hold her in my arms; but more often I was oppressed by nightmares in which Wauglan Waud would loom mighty as a thundercloud, with his square jaws, hard brown agates of eyes, and mustache twirling upward to enormous points. Then, in more lucid intervals, this terrifying image would give place to the placid form of Yutir, who sat at my side, smiling encouragingly.

As my strength flowed back to me, Captain Orfgu assigned me to work. After learning the code, which was very simple, I was put in charge of the signalling, and had to transmit messages to other ships and to islands and ports by means of colored flags during the day, and colored lights at night. Yutir meanwhile, because of his keen eyes and nautical experience, was given the duties of a *Turgin* or minor officer, which he enjoyed immensely as his huge form went bustling about, inspiring respect from all the men.

After stops at various small ports, we came to the fabled Cocoanut Islands, including lovely Zuttel, whose inhabitants, for reasons of "Supreme Secrecy," were being evacuated to homes several days' sailing away. As for smaller Hilos—we were not permitted near it at all, because of a Government project, also of "Supreme Secrecy."

As I stood staring out at Zuttel's mountain crowned shores, lined with cocoanut groves and brilliant with orchids, my mind went back to an incident of long before; I heard once more the arrogant Wauglan Waud: ". . . we can work from Hilos, drive an experimental tunnel to Zuttel toward the active volcano, and cause an eruption. . . . After this, Zuttel will be a nursery for the fishes."

Was there still time to prevent this catastrophe? If I could only bring the *Kolem* my information as to the progress of the experiments of the Eastern Islanders!

It seemed much later when, after a long, uneventful voyage, Captain Orfgu summoned Yutir and me to his cabin.

"Tomorrow we reach Kallendra," he reported, a glitter in his keen brown eyes as he stood bowlegged on the shaking deck. "You've both been good seamen. I want to take you on our next cruise. I can offer two Atlantids a day—"

I saw the joy on Yutir's beaked, reddish face.

"Captain Orfgu," he said, lifting his left hand high overhead in the accustomed seaman's salute, "the gods intended me for the sea. I thank the stars for the privilege of staying with you."

The Captain grunted approval. And now two pairs

149

of eyes were fixed expectantly upon me. Do not think that I was not tempted. Life on the *Green Turtle* had been pleasant, and my bond to Yutir had tightened into deep friendship.

"The gods will reward you for your generosity, Captain Orfgu," I said, saluting. "Unhappily, they command me to return to Kallendra."

The Captain bowed, his dark eyes narrowing with disappointment. Yutir shook his head sadly. But both accepted my decision.

A more affecting moment followed, when I took leave of Yutir. "Sometime surely, when your ship comes into port again, old friend, we'll meet once more," I foretold.

However, there was much to excite me now, as I found myself once more in Kallendra. To think that Lampra was sharing this very air! We would meet again—yes, not even Argillon and the she-witch Testa could keep us apart!

A deep-seated uneasiness came over me when I stood once more on the sea-facing avenue, the *Cruzzo*, from which five years before, I had stolen off like a hunted animal. True, I was not likely to be recognized now, with my green sailor's tunic, the heavily grizzled growth that covered my face, the deep seams and trenches on my forehead. None the less, my first act was to purchase a pair of dark green glasses by way of further disguise. And my next step was to hire a *litto*.

If I had followed my impulses, I would have flown straight to Lampra. But I was not quite that reckless. I must learn the lay of the land before deciding on my strategy. Meanwhile, I must see my old friend Langhis Ghand, whom I had remembered so many a time with deep affection.

Somehow, I was disappointed as I guided my *litto* through the familiar streets. They seemed different

150

than of old. Was it not true that the people on the streets were more hurried and worried than five summers ago, the buildings dingier and grimier, and the *littos* not quite so bright colored? On the *Cordocco,* I was shocked to see that many of the shrubs and flowers were withering.

But the *Klar,* or viewing screen, still stared as of old from its blank yellowish-white wall; and crowds, much larger than of old, stood as if fascinated, gazing at the large moving letters flashed from a distant reflector by the Central Information Service, the *Drust.* Though impatient to reach Langhis, I could not help joining the crowd.

The words, however, only confused me. ". . . another of the disturbances. The shock is reported as of magnitude 918, less severe than some of the others. The residents of a wide area were shaken. There have been widely scattered reports of noises. The authorities hold that there is nothing here except normal seismic manifestations. . . ."

"Normal seismic manifestations—my foot!" I heard someone muttering. "These troubles have been going on a whole year now, getting worse all the time. They're all due to those tigers from the Eastern Isles."

"My belief, too!" agreed a second bystander. "Those wild beasts have planted spies, ready to blow us all up. You should see the crack back of my house!"

"I've lived seventy-nine summers, and never have I seen anything like it," resumed the first speaker. "But what's that?"

". . . the situation has been deteriorating," I read on the *Klar.* "The *Magnonem* of the Eastern Isles still refuses the apology demanded by our *Kolem,* and claims that any violation of territory was on our part. Meanwhile a concentration of our underwater forces has been announced in the Wendrian Gulf. The *thungsibgia* or fireball-hurlers are said to have been put in secret launching sites."

"The gods preserve us! Looks like war!" I heard one man bewailing, as I started away.

I would gladly have remained to hear more, but my growing uneasiness bade me be on my way again.

Half an hour later, I approached Langhis' home on the lower slopes of Mt. Nublis. The neighborhood was still serene and lovely, but I gave little thought to the sights. My heart beat wildly as I knocked at a remembered door.

A few seconds passed. Then I heard footsteps within.

As the door opened, I stared into the round-cheeked face of Wulta, the wife of Langhis. Not answering my greeting, she stared back without recognition, and even, I thought, with hostility.

"May I—may I see Langhis? Say it's—an old friend."

She scanned me from hair to toes. I thought she would shut the door in my face. Then she mumbled, "I'll see if he can come," and without inviting me in, slipped out of view.

Several minutes went by. I could hear her voice. "... nothing but a ragged sailor ... claims to be an old friend."

"No doubt ... wants a handout," the answer came in my friend's clear tones.

Another minute passed. Then Langhis stood before me, his candid big eyes surveying me with a puzzled stare.

"Langhis!"

His face was convulsed with astonishment and joy. "Klantor!" he shouted. And he clapped his arms about me.

It was minutes before we could talk coherently. Then I noticed that his eyes were moist.

"Come in," he requested.

Once inside, he held me at arm's length and peered at me with those tranquil, kindly eyes. "You—you will forgive me, Klantor, for not recognizing you. You are so changed. Where, in the name of great Ablum, have you been?"

"I have thought of you so often, Langhis. Has all been well?"

"Thanks to the gods, all has been well. Be seated, Klantor," he invited, pointing to a heap of cushions in a corner. "Let us have a little *mevot.*"

Nervously he rushed to an inner door, and called to his wife.

"Yes, all has been well. And how about you? Tell me all that's happened to you, Klantor."

"More has happened than I could recite in many days," I answered. And just then Wulta entered with a tray holding the sweet drink or *lipopu* and the date-cakes and other dainties that made up the *mevot.*

After she had gone and I had told in swift outline of the events of the past five years, Langhis bent forward on his pile of cushions, pointed one long, lean finger at me in his old way, and suggested, "Now I suppose you're anxious for the news?"

"Anxious? I'm famished."

He pursed up his lips. "Then you know nothing of the disturbances?"

"Well, passing through the *Romul,* I gathered that you've had some earthquakes."

"Earthquakes indeed!" Langhis' eyes widened owlishly. "And what earthquakes! By the rings of Saturn! they've toppled towers, cracked walls and embankments, broken water mains and sewers, and even killed some people."

"But we've had earthquakes before."

"Never anything like these. As far back as the records go—more than three hundred years—we've had nothing remotely approaching these shocks that have come one after another, rocking us until at times, Klantor, the ground beneath us has seemed like a wave at sea. What worries me is that the general pattern has changed."

"Do scientists see any reason?"

"Oh, yes. They attribute it to the volcanoes—subterranean stirrings."

"Why should there all at once be subterranean stirrings?"

Langhis threw up his hands in a helpless gesture. Then suddenly I was struck by an idea so startling, so dreadful that I may have winced, for Langhis gasped, "Why, what's wrong, Klantor?"

"Nothing, I hope," I answered, slowly, still shaken. "But don't any scientists think of a possibility other than spontaneous underground stirrings?"

"What other possibility can there be?"

"Maybe I'm wrong—I pray to great Ablum that I am. But after what I've heard at meetings of the *Kolem*—and seen on the island of Zug—I can think of other reasons for the disturbances."

I bent over my friend, and poured out my suspicions in an agitated torrent.

"Suppose—just suppose that the Eastern Islanders decided to bore a secret submarine tunnel from the Fernaz Peninsula, so as to let in the sea water and start an eruption. They could gain access without any trouble, since the region is fog-crowned nine tenths of the time; and they could come disguised as fishermen. Since their work would be mostly underground, they would elude detection—"

"But what of the excavated materials?"

"They could dump those into the sea at night. I tell you, Langhis, from my experience at Project J, I know it's all feasible, and the more plausible since there's fresh danger of war with the Eastern Isles. The jarring and dislocation of unstable earth-strata would explain the rumblings, the earthquake shocks, the subsidence of the land—especially if they're excavating by means of powerful explosives to save time."

Why was it that just at this moment, the words of the Seeress of the Dawn once more came back to my mind?—"Small storms precede great! Small storms precede great!"

"I must tell the *Kolem* what I know," I went on. "I can attend one of their public sessions—well disguised. If Wulta didn't recognize me and you had trouble, it isn't likely, is it, that any of the Councillors would identify me—that is, unless Argillon—"

I halted in mid-sentence, for I noticed the peculiar expression on Langhis' face.

"Argillon?" he answered my unspoken question, with a slow, emphatic utterance. "You have nothing more, Klantor, to fear from Argillon. Two summers ago, a fresh heart attack sent him back to his ancestors."

So I should never again see Argillon's familiar figure! "May the gods be kind to him!" I expressed the conventional wish for the dead.

But it was not chiefly of Argillon that I was thinking. It was of Lampra. "And what of his daughter?" I jerked out. "How has she fared?"

"What are you all so pale and agitated about, Klantor?" Langhis asked. "So far as I've heard, Lampra is still unwed. I assume she is living in her father's old home—"

"May Ablum grant that you're right! I'll be going to her now!" I suddenly decided, starting toward the door.

He was staring across at me with indulgent eyes. "When will you be back?"

"Oh, in two or three days, old friend—"

Langhis tossed his head back in a hearty laugh. "Do

you think I'll be put off that long? Oh, no, you'll be back this very night—and stay with us as long as you wish. Now that Cleone's married, we have a spare room, which is yours. Come, come—don't thank me—and don't refuse!" he deterred, noting my half-uttered protests. "After all, you owe something to old friendship. Now may the gods bless you and Lampra!"

CHAPTER XXIV

LAMPRA

As I entered Argillon's grounds, I had a sharp sense of change. The grass had turned brown, and many of the flowers and shrubs had withered, as in other parts of Kallendra, owing to the breaking of water mains by the earthquake.

Wearing my green glasses, I stole in by a rear approach. Oh, if only I could avoid being recognized But as I made a sharp turn around some bushes, I almost ran into a spade-bearing figure. Though he was grayer and stooped more than of old, I knew him at once. Ru Manir, the gardener!

He looked at me without recognition.

"May the gods bless your day, sir," he uttered the conventional greeting. With a nod, I passed on, my heart thumping. If Ru Manir recognized me, then

157

there would be no further safety for me in Kallendra.

But since the old gardener did not know me, surely that she-vulture, Testa, would not. Nevertheless, I trembled as I reached the irised seven-fountained court and climbed the sandstone steps to the great bronze door of the mansion. On the verandah, I hesitated just a moment to give my pounding heart a chance. Then I reached up and pulled the brass door-clapper.

It was only seconds before I heard footsteps inside —seconds that were age-long. Should I at last be face to face with my beloved?

But no! A strange young woman, with a round pleasant face, looked at me inquiringly.

"Is—is Miss Lampra in?"

"What name shall I give?"

My fingers shook uncontrollably. However, I did somehow find the small envelope hidden in my inner garments.

"Give her this, my girl, and the gods bless you. I'll wait for the answer."

I had enclosed a notation that would be intelligible to none but Lampra: our old-time symbol, "X * * * X."

The servant received the envelope doubtfully, and shut the door upon me, leaving me to shift nervously from leg to leg.

Several epochs went by. Finally, I heard footsteps again. Now, surely, it was Lampra! But no! as the door opened, I stared once more into the servant's round puzzled face.

"The mistress says come in."

A moment later, I was in a remembered room of seaweed tapestries with the shaded light filtering in through the emerald-green windows.

"Have the kindness to wait here," said the servant, and bowed her way out. Then all at once I saw a door

158

bursting open; saw an apparition facing me in the subdued light—Lampra, as beautiful as ever, with a mature loveliness, her coppery hair bunched as of old above her shining broad forehead, her fire-filled dark little eyes wide with wonder.

Overpowered by joy, I started toward her. "Lampra!"

But she merely stared—stared hard at me, in a bewildered way. And something froze my steps.

"Lampra! Precious one! Don't you know me?"

At these words, the barrier melted away.

"Klantor!" she screamed. With a rush, she was in my arms.

How long we clung together, mingling our tears, is more than I will ever be able to say. It was minutes before we could even hold one another at arm's length.

"You're just the same as ever, precious one," I testi-fied, though I did detect a new sadness in her eyes, and a new firmness about her lips.

"And you—you, Klantor, look so different! What terrible things you must have gone through! Oh, promise me, promise you'll never go away from me again!"

"Never! By the gods, never!" I swore.

"Oh, I can't help feeling, maybe—maybe you're just like that other one!" she broke out, passionately. And she clasped me tightly, as if to make sure I was of solid flesh. "That other one who wasn't really there!"

"What other one?"

Through tears that still dimmed her eyes, she went on.

"It was at that terrible city of Admenebda. There was a dreadful riot, and just before the riot I saw you—oh, I'm sure I saw you right in the front of the crowd, though Father only laughed and said I was dreaming. But I know it was you—your good spirit, Klantor, sent there to save me from the rioters—"

"It was not only my spirit, precious one. I myself was there and did try to shield you," I answered. "I'll explain. First, what have you to tell me?"

"Oh, my life has been a level plain," she reported. "Except, of course—you know about Father?"

"Yes, Lampra, I have heard the sad news," I acknowledged; and expressed my sympathy. And then, after a decent interval, "And what about your old servant, Testa?"

"Oh, Testa? I've found a maid who's better suited to me. But let's not think about Testa!" With suddenly increased fervor, she drew me nearer. "Always, always, Klantor, I was waiting for you! Always I had faith the gods would bring us together! Father—he would mock me. He tried so hard to make me marry! Father was very angry when I refused."

"Bless you for that, Lampra! I too have waited, waited so long! Five whole summers, and I couldn't even send a message for fear of betraying myself!"

Sudden fear crossed Lampra's face. Impulsively she slipped out of my arms, dashed to the door, and opened it to make sure that no one was eavesdropping.

"Priceless one, are you sure you're safe?" she exclaimed, as she darted back to me. "Have the charges been dismissed?"

"I wish I could believe so."

She clasped me again; clung to me as if she would never let me go.

"There was a great commotion when you disappeared," she went on. "I don't know all about it, but I've heard the whole country was stirred up. They were looking for you everywhere on a charge of treason. I knew you were hiding somewhere. Oh, how I prayed to the gods! They did hear me, too!"

160

"Otherwise, I wouldn't be here now."

"But are you safe? Are you safe even yet?" she cried, while she glanced about her as if afraid that pursuers would burst in. "How—how under the stars did you get here? Maybe it's not safe, Klantor, for you to go out into the street. You can stay here, well hidden, until—"

I drew her close; soothed her with kisses; explained that I felt well protected by my changed appearance; mentioned that I had promised to stay with Langhis. And then, after telling in barest outline of my adventures, "There's not been a day of all these many days, precious one, when I have not dreamed of joining our lives. When shall the time be?"

Her face reddened. Her fingers fluttered. Slowly and simply, she said, "I too have dreamed of this many and many a day. Let the time be whenever you wish."

Unhappily, I was still a hunted man—and before the law would permit me to marry, I must mention my name, and consequently would be more likely to go to a dungeon than to the nuptial chamber. And an assumed name might bring on a risky investigation.

"I've thought of all this carefully, precious one," I reported. "There is only one possibility."

Wide-mouthed, she stared at me. And just then I felt a sharp swaying beneath us. The divan slid forward as if on rollers; the walls began to heave, shake, and rattle, like a cabin in rough weather at sea; I heard distant crashes and rumblings; and a huge tapestry on the wall, with a sudden swish, slipped down and half buried us. Many seconds passed before we disentangled ourselves and the quaking ceased.

"By Ablum! That was a bad one!" I muttered. "Are you hurt, Lampra?"

"No—not except here," she testified, pressing one hand against her heart. "These shocks, they've been

161

coming so often, they're tearing my nerves to tatters."

"Listen, precious one!" I hastened on, eagerly. "How would you like to go with me, to live on one of the most beautiful islands in all the nine seas, where you wouldn't fear these shocks? Ever heard of Ajaka?"

"Ajaka? Oh, yes, of course! A lovely place of blue seas, sunshine, and flowers!"

"I once stopped there. Since it's independent of both the Western Isles and the Eastern, I'd be safe there. Both of us—we'd be happy. However, it's many days' sail from here. I've been puzzling how to get there."

Lampra's face broke into a sudden bloom of joy. She clapped her hands together. "By the gods, priceless one, that isn't any problem at all!"

I stared at her inquiringly.

"Why, what of the *Coral Reef*, Father's pleasure ship? He always said it was good and seaworthy, and he's left it to me! It's down at a private dock, and will have to be overhauled—which will take time."

"After all these years, what if it does take a little longer?" I philosophized. "Meanwhile, I have a mission here in Kallendra. Let's thank the gods, Lampra, for your ship!"

"Thank the gods!" she repeated. "I'll see Father's agent tomorrow."

"Good! And the captain will marry us as soon as we're out of Western waters!" I proposed, enthusiastically. "But are you sure, Lampra, you have the means?"

"Means?" She threw back her head, with its shock of coppery curls, and laughed deliciously. "Why, Father left me more Atlantids than I know what to do with!"

But even as she threw out her arms once more, and I clasped her warm, convulsive form, a voice of warn-

162

ing seemed to call out in my ears. Again the insinuating tones of the Seeress of the Dawn came to me. "Small storms precede great! Small storms precede great! Small storms precede great!"

CHAPTER XXV

THE MADMAN FROM
THE EASTERN ISLES

Absorbed in adjusting the hand telescope, I did not notice as Langhis opened the door of my room in his house. Hearing a grunt, I looked up to see him staring darkly at me.

"What is it?" I gasped. "Not feeling sick?"

"No, it's the whole lunatic world that's sick," he answered, wrily, as he dropped to a seat on some cushions at my side. "Haven't heard the latest?"

"What latest?"

"According to reports on the *Klar*, we've recalled our negotiators from the Eastern Isles. We blame them for the impasse; they blame us; and both sides prepare fireball-hurlers and send out undersea fighting fleets."

"Then you think, Langhis, it will be war?"

He groaned.

"But by the red light of Mars! It's all absurd!" I said, dolefully shaking my head. "Why, having been in the Eastern Isles, I know we're as much alike as twins! The people—you couldn't tell them from our own. I'll never forget how Kimpoc rescued me. And Yutir, who was like a brother to me after my escape—"

I broke short; mention of Yutir had brought back remembrance of the experiments in volcanic warfare. "By Ablum!" I burst out. "We must do something to prevent catastrophe!"

. "In this case, everything is nothing," Langhis diagnosed gloomily. "We might as soon try to stop the tides. But surely you won't go to that affair tomorrow?"

He was referring, of course, to the meeting of the *Kolem*, which I had awaited ever since my return to Kallendra. At this session, when the public was invited to express its views, I might at last reveal the dread preparations of the Eastern Islanders.

"No, Langhis," I said, firmly, "there's more reason than ever for me to go to the meeting."

Suddenly he was on his feet. One of his arms was around my shoulders. "Come, come, old friend, haven't you sacrificed enough already? You could as soon budge Mt. Nublis as those mules of Councillors."

"Only a rabbit-heart," I protested, "refuses to fight just because the battle will be hard."

"No one, Klantor, would call you a rabbit-heart. But consider this," he rushed on, his hands shaking in nervous haste. "Thus far you've been lucky. Ever since your return I've trembled for fear some accident would tear off your disguise. So why press your luck? Why take the risk someone will recognize you—"

"I've been practicing to disguise my voice. There won't be any clue."

"There are *always* clues. But even if you don't care one wink for your own safety, don't you owe it to Lampra to protect yourself?"

I sighed. "Lampra wouldn't want me to betray everything I've ever fought for."

Though I would hardly admit it to myself, I did know that to influence the *Kolem* would be like moving mountains. But having dreamed for years of coming before this body and reporting the secrets I had learned, could I back out now?

"Very well, then," Langhis conceded after a time. "If you insist on ramming your nose into a stone wall, I'll go with you tomorrow."

And then, with a rapid change of subject: "Have you seen Lampra today?"

"No day passes without my seeing her," I answered, with a smile; and hurried on, enthusiastically, "You should see how she's been blooming."

"How are the plans for the *Coral Reef* getting on?"

"The ship is almost completely fitted out and provisioned. And what a sleek beauty she is! Lampra's agent has hired a captain and most of the crew. With luck, we can sail in five or six days."

"Oh! So soon? Well, Klantor, you know how sorry I'll be to lose you. But for your sake, I'll lift my arms and thank all the gods that you're safely off our soil."

I laughed. "Have no fear, old friend!" But I felt a persistent, nagging uneasiness.

Strangely, this uneasiness clung to me next morning, when Langhis and I traveled to the *Hall of the Kolem.* I had a queer, sinking sensation to see again that large, low building. And my gloom only deepened when I was again inside the Golden Conclave Hall with its colored light strips, its walls with the images of great war machines, and the motto of the Western Confederacy standing out in letters of flame: *Light, Liberty, and Learning.*

The hall was nearly full as Langhis and I entered and climbed to the top row. I was wearing a plain dark brown tunic; and I was convinced that this, along with my green glasses and grizzled full beard, made me into a completely different man from the youthful, clean-shaven Klantor Fey.

Not long after my arrival, a small side door opened, and the nine *Kolem* filed in. I could not join in the uproarious cheers that dinned all about me.

After a time, however, I did bring myself to glance at the Councillors seated about the pale rose lacquered table at one end of the great hall. I saw Wauglan Waud, his square face looking squarer and more seamed and soured than ever as he sat in arrogant majesty in second place, in Argillon's old seat. At the head of the table, even more withered than of old, I recognized the priest-leader Drandro-dra. But old white-haired Velto Vanrr, the representative of the *Clotilla*, was not to be seen; nor was Dr. Zuno Klan. In the seat I had once occupied, I observed a staid-looking graybeard.

The past seemed to spring back to life when Drandro-dra summoned two black basalt figures out of a hidden niche, and prostrated himself in prayer: "O Ablum! O Quag-ulta! God and goddess of the earth and heavens! Once more we place ourselves in your power! . . ."

In an awed silence, the audience listened. Then with a sigh, Drandro-dra turned from the idols. The stare of his pewter eyes passed beyond his fellow Councillors to the breathlessly waiting spectators. And again I heard his mealy voice:

"My brothers of the *Kolem!* Sons and daughters of the Western Isles! The *Kolem* being meant to serve the people, we hold meetings now and then at which any citizen may express his views. All regular business

167

will be suspended today while you, my fellow Western Islanders, may speak your minds. It is well that you do so now, for we face a great crisis; the insolent Eastern Islanders threaten us by land and sea. As you may have heard, they have mounted batteries of those dread weapons, the *thungsibgia,* on their western shores. But our military command will meet the threat!"

Waud puffed out his broad chest, and sat looking fierce and haughty.

"Now for the day's business!" Drandro-dra went on. "Remember, there are many to be heard. Who will be first?"

Instantly I was on my feet. But so were a score of others; I was not noticed, while a weedy-looking man in the front row was heard concerning the need for increasing the speed limit for *littos.* Many others followed, and all the while my impatience and anxiety were rising. Twenty times I was on my feet, demanding the right to be heard. But twenty times I was overlooked. Toward the end, however, the competition was greatly diminished. So many had been heard that only five or six were seeking the chairman's attention when at last he announced, "We've time for just one more!" and pointed a bony finger at me. "You, my friend back there in the top row!"

As I sprang out of my seat, I was conscious of the hundreds of pairs of eyes that turned toward me from every part of the packed hall. A second went by; the glaring light strips danced and wavered before me. Then, remembering the need to disguise my voice, I spoke in squeaky, high-pitched tones.

"Respected *Kolem!* Honored fellow citizens! My name is Munjin Alg. The reason I came here—"

I was interrupted by a rumbling from beneath my feet. Suddenly the floor began to shake; I was swaying and pitching so violently that I had to clutch the back of a chair to keep my balance. Shouts and screams came from all directions as the building rocked and the golden light strips flickered; men and women started out of their seats and began crowding into the aisles.

Then, as abruptly as it had begun, the disturbance was over. Drandro-dra, waving his arms in excited gestures, motioned the audience back to their places. "Sons and daughters of the Western Isles! There is nothing to fear! This is just another of those little tremors, which, scientists assure us, are caused by slight internal readjustments of the earth. They are certain to diminish. Let us go on with our business!"

I steadied myself, and tried not to notice that the floor was again trembling.

"Estimable *Kolem*! Respected fellow citizens!" I resumed, abandoning my rehearsed approach. "The small shock you have just felt will tell you why I am here. I believe I have discovered the cause. I have here some computations which will prove that I have something more than a theory!"

For the sake of effect, I paused.

But this gave the chairman his opportunity to ask, "And what, my good friend, is this providentially discovered cause of the shocks?"

Spectators in various parts of the hall burst into titters.

"The facts, respected fellow citizens, are these," I hurried on. "Our enemies of the Eastern Isles, by boring secretly beneath the sea or bay, to tap the sources of subterranean energy—"

A low ripple of laughter, starting in a far corner, swiftly gained volume.

"And just how," demanded Drandro-dra, his voice

icily sarcastic, "are our enemies to accomplish this simple feat?"

I could see the amused smiles on dozens of faces.

"Worthy Chairman," I answered, growing angrier, "I do not call it a simple feat to bore beneath the sea or bay. But it can be done. Under clever disguises, the Eastern Islanders may be undermining the very ground we stand on."

Again that low ripple of laughter.

"Only listen, noble *Kolem!*" I pleaded, once more waving my papers. "This all involves technical matters, difficult to explain. But I have here the full facts, diagrams, analyses, and computations. If you will subject them to scrutiny by scientists—"

Again that disconcerting laughter. From somewhere across the hall, there came a hilarious outburst. "Madman! Madman!" And from the opposite side, the words were repeated, "Madman! Madman! Madman!"

"My friend," Drandro-dra demanded, still in the same cutting tones, "do you imagine no scientist has ever scrutinized the facts? You seem to forget that our defenses are in charge of the celebrated Wauglan Waud, who has left not a pebble untouched. Is that not so, honorable Waud?"

Waud nodded, and answered in the scratching tones I so well remembered. "Never, revered Drandro-dra, was any country better defended than the Western Isles."

"And so, my friend in the rear row, have you anything more to say?" demanded the chairman.

"Only this, esteemed *Kolem.* I have never questioned the defenses of the country. But the recent earthquakes may not be due to natural causes—"

"Neither may the lightning, hurricane, or fiery meteor!" Drandro-dra broke in mockingly.

Again the laughter, this time in a torrent. And again the cry, "Madman! Madman!" was taken up by

170

hundreds of voices and shrilled about my ears in a storm.

"Fellow citizens," I burst out above the chorus of jeers, "a man is not mad because he proposes a new scientific explanation. If you will let me tell of my experiences in the Eastern Isles—"

"By the gods, you've told too much already! Time's up!" the chairman interrupted, while the laughter continued, along with the hoots of "Madman! Madman!"

In the midst of the ensuing prayers, another earthquake shook the hall, and the crowd began pushing its way out. But I did not miss the smirks and grimaces as I tried to leave at Langhis' side; I could not help hearing the mutterings and gibes. "Madman! Madman! There goes the madman!"

When at last we were in the open again, Langhis sighed, then turned to me with a smile meant to be reassuring. "Thanks to great Ablum, that wasn't as bad as I expected."

Nevertheless, I was feeling as if the whole sky had come down about my shoulders. My long-awaited appearance before the *Kolem* had ended in blank failure.

As this bleak thought obsessed me, the very pavement seemed to turn liquid in one of the most severe earthquakes yet; columns and cornices thundered down all about me.

"Well, Langhis old friend, the gods will bless you for coming with me today," I said, as we regained our *littos*. "Now I'm going straight to Lampra."

"It's just noon," he answered, consulting the timerod concealed inside his tunic. "Remember, this evening Wulta and I will expect Lampra and you. We're looking forward to this little wedding celebration."

"Lampra and I wouldn't miss it, Langhis."

171

As I started away, with the earth beneath me again rumbling and grumbling, I had no idea how near we were to our last act in Kallendra.

CHAPTER XXVI

THE FLAMING DRAGON

As soon as we saw Langhis, Lampra and I knew that something was wrong. He stood in front of his house, awaiting us, but he looked grim and troubled.

We too were troubled. The earthquakes, continuing all afternoon, had jarred our nerves, as had the ominous turn the weather had taken, with a sultry, oppressive heaviness beneath the rainless, lead-gray clouds.

"Come in!" said Langhis, rather hurriedly. Inside the house, Wulta also received us gravely, with no evidence of the expected festive spirit. I was surprised not to see any of the bright lamps, the gauds and tinsels that usually marked a celebration.

"Sit down, my friends!" Langhis invited, with an unhappy grimace.

The women and I seated ourselves. But Langhis remained standing.

A jarring earthquake intervened. Then my friend burst out, "Listen, people! It torments me to say it, but we'd better give up our little party."

"By great Ablum, Langhis, what is it?" I demanded, springing up. "It hasn't anything to do with that meeting this morning?"

Langhis gritted his teeth. "Unfortunately it *has* to do with that meeting. Remember how alarmed I was?"

"Out with it, please. It isn't—it isn't—they haven't—" I stammered, with visions of being seized by the Public Protectors.

"No—they haven't identified you—at least, I believe not. But unhappily, they have identified *me*."

"You?" I shouted, in stunned amazement.

"Me—I had the indiscretion to be seen with you, Klantor . . . No don't misunderstand me," he hastily added. "It's nothing to damage me personally. But you made yourself conspicuous, as you know, and were seen in my company."

"Being Head Star Watcher," Wulta put in, with a fond glance at her husband, "Langhis is naturally known everywhere."

"But what is it? What under the stars?" I demanded.

Lampra rose and put one hand confidently in mine. "Whatever it is, Klantor, we'll share it—"

"First better learn what it is!" Langhis warned. "Early this afternoon, I had a call from two strangers —blunt, burly men, who said they were his friends."

"*My* friends?"

"However, they didn't give your name as Klantor, but as Mujin Alg. So I knew they'd heard your name at the meeting today. They wanted to know where to find you. I said that great Ablum alone knew. Then they asked when you would be here. I swore you'd be gone all the rest of the day, and tomorrow, and the day after. But I knew they didn't believe me. They promised to be back soon. I'd take my oath they *will* be back."

"It's easy to see," I muttered, "they're Public Protectors!"

"Anyhow," Langhis rushed on, "they asked a great many questions. Do you ever suffer from delusions? Do you have false ideas of grandeur? Are you known for your eccentric notions? Have you a fear of persecution?"

"In other words," I broke out, sharply, "am I crazy?"

Langhis shook his head glumly. "That's just it. They wanted you for the Hospital for Mental Incurables."

"Oh, no, no, no, that couldn't be!" I heard Lampra's voice, high-pitched with terror. "There's—there's some mistake!"

"So I too thought," conceded Langhis, standing with arms sternly folded, "But I decided to make sure."

"How?"

Suddenly the room shook with such fury that the windows rattled.

Langhis waited for the quake to die down, then went on. "I knew, of course, that those men had given me false names. As soon as they'd left, therefore, I rushed for my *litto*, and followed them halfway across the city, always keeping far enough behind not to be noticed amid the traffic. My suspicions were confirmed by the direction they headed in. Finally, they left their *littos*—guess where?"

"In front of the Hospital for Mental Incurables!"

Langhis mumbled an affirmative.

"So, Klantor, I knew I must warn you. At Lampra's, the maid said you were not there, and she didn't

175

know when you'd be back. I left a message asking you to come here immediately."

"We'd gone down to see the *Coral Reef*," explained Lampra. "We were so interested! The Captain and some of the crew were showing us how nearly ready she was."

"Thank the gods!" Langhis exclaimed. Darting to the door, he peered out suspiciously. "Come! Better get away!"

"But what are we to do? What, in the name of Quag-ulta?" Lampra appealed, staring all about her wildly. "Poor Klantor! You've been through so much!"

Just then another earthquake, which sent objects crashing to the floor, gave a new turn to our thoughts.

"Listen, people!" Langhis took up, hammering the air with one fist. "There's only one way out. Lampra! is your boat ready?"

"We hadn't really expected—not for several days yet," she faltered. "Still, if—if the Captain can make it—I'd feel a thousand times safer at sea!"

"We'd all feel safer. The Captain will have to make it!" insisted Langhis. "Come! Let's go!"

Another earthquake followed, so severe that the translucent dome of the living room split jaggedly with a wrenching sound.

"The gods preserve us! Will we ever come out of this alive?" wailed Wulta, staring at the gap in the ceiling.

"But we can't—can't go right to the boat!" exclaimed Lampra, throwing up both arms distractedly. "I haven't a thing with me. Besides, I can't leave my maid Uletta. First I must go to my house!"

"Wulta and I will go with you," volunteered Langhis, as he threw open the door. "We'll see you to the docks."

An earthquake almost shook us off our feet as we trailed away into the twilight. A thick layer of cloud,

176

granite-gray, inky-blue, and muddy-yellow, covered the sky, especially deep about the summit of Mt. Nublis, which was wreathed in coppery vapors, from which white lightnings flashed continually, varied by ruddy flickers and flares. The atmosphere was warm and heavy.

Speechlessly, we all took to our *littos*, but as we started away, there was one continuous earthquake, the ground trembling incessantly. Through the murky half-light, I saw how pale my companions looked, with set, grim faces, and staring, apprehensive eyes.

Then, from somewhere in the distance, there came the din of an explosion. This was followed, after a few seconds, by an even louder commotion; and the ground beneath us seemed to be tilted by a giant hand and to sink half an arm's length.

But this was nothing compared to the sights above. "Nublis! Nublis!" we cried, pointing. The mists over the mountain had been rifted by shafts of orange-red.

Then out of every doorway the people began pouring with shouts and yells. "Nublis! Nublis! Nublis!" From far away, merging with this screaming chorus, there rose a long-drawn wailing of many voices. Some people got down on hands and knees, others lifted wild arms in prayer. Dogs barked, doves and gulls wheeled about in panicky flights, children bawled, and women called out with shrill, frightened cries. Soon there came a third explosion, louder than the others, and the fires about the peak were muffled by tremendous whitish mists, through which, intermittently, the flames could still be seen in rosy and golden puffs.

Keeping as close together as we could, the four of us glided on our *littos* through the shuddering streets. The streetlamps were disquietingly dark. In the houses there was no light except for occasional candles. But we could see our way well enough by means

177

of the blue, white, and golden lightnings that clove the heavens and the fiery clouds.

Minute by minute, meanwhile, the atmosphere was thickening. An irritating, acrid smell—the suffocating reek of sulphur—was in the air. At the same time, a fine rain of cinders began falling all about us on a rising wind.

We had to move slowly now, for people were dashing about the streets in all directions, not seeming to know where. We had to avoid the cracks that had opened up in the streets, some of them wide enough to catch the wheels of our *littos*.

Yet, through all this horror, I moved with the fatalistic feeling that it was something I had foreseen, foreknown. That Mt. Nublis, supposedly long extinct, should suddenly erupt—this seemed but part of the inexorable fate. Somehow, with a sense deeper than reason, I knew that worse lay ahead.

All during this ghastly pilgrimage, I tried not to lose sight of Lampra, tried to reassure her by my presence, by a touch, by a nod. Whenever I came near, I could feel her whole form fluttering. Nor were things improved when we reached her home.

By the quivering light, we saw that a long stone wall was broken in several places; rocks larger than a man's head had tumbled down. A tall palm tree slanted crazily. The sandstone steps were cracked, and the porch was leaning like a storm-bent cedar.

At the door, Uletta met us with a plastic oil lamp. "Thanks be to the gods, mistress, you're back at last!" she cried, fervently. "I thought by Quag-ulta, you'd be killed!

"Everything's been tumbling down!" she rushed on, when the closed door had muffled the outside noises. "The dishes in the kitchen—they're all broken. There are so many cracks in the walls and ceiling I can't even count them."

178

A series of detonations from outside, like distant thunder, drew nearer until they seemed to boom directly beneath our feet.

Lampra turned to me a face which, in the dim lamplight, looked strained and taut. "What do you think it can be, Klantor?"

"I'm afraid, precious one, it's the diabolical thing I've been fighting against. Now that there's no secret to hide, I can tell you that something like this was planned by us against the Eastern Isles. They've struck first!"

"Planned?" wailed Lampra. "You mean—"

Langhis broke in impatiently. "Come, come, there's no time for words! You can't get to that boat too fast!"

A severe tremor emphasized this idea, making us clutch at a table for support.

"Just a few things—I'll get just a few things!" Lampra rattled out. And having lighted a second plastic lamp, she set off with Uletta. They both returned remarkably soon, each clutching a half-filled bag. "I—I'm afraid to go up the stairs!" Lampra confessed. "They—they're so twisted—"

As she spoke, the whole house shook once more. The roaring outside had increased to a howling fury against which we had to struggle to make ourselves heard.

"Uletta, you're to come, too—on the boat!" Lampra almost shrieked.

"Thanks be to the gods, mistress!"

"And what of Langhis and Wulta?" I cried.

"The gods will take care of us," answered Langhis.

"No, you'll both come!" Lampra threw out. Then, carrying the plastic lamps and the bags, we started toward the door.

Outside, the tumult had grown. The continuous roaring, as of a gigantic furnace, was louder than ever. The clouds over most of the sky were of an un-

179

earthly bronze; but around the peak of Nublis they showed a deep ruddy hue, lit by continuous sheet lightning. The wind had increased, and so had the sulphurous fumes; the air was hotter than ever, with a dry searing heat against which we could not protect ourselves.

We advanced with a snail's speed, forced to discard our *littos*, which were useless in the growing darkness. Back and forth, all about us, more haphazardly than ever, the fugitives were drifting, a few carrying lamps or candles, but most relying upon the fitful light of the heavens. From among my nightmarish recollections of that night-journey, I have pictures of mothers with babes slung over their backs, crazily clutching the hands of wailing urchins; families trundling bundles on small three-wheeled carts; shrieking children wandering about, crying for their parents; aged folk hobbling along; demented persons racing about in circles, or beating against bare walls; quaking men and women bowing to small images of gods they carried in their hands.

All the while, the crashing of the elements was matched by the noise of falling chimneys and columns. To avoid being hit, we tried to keep to the middle of the street. And so as not to be separated, we joined hands.

As we staggered forward, we had to pass through the *Romul* or central square, which was packed with squirming, threshing people. Here alone the city's lighting remained, fed by emergency batteries; on the *Klar*, messages were being flashed, while multitudes stood watching and muttering.

Eager for information, we squeezed forward until we could make out the words on the tall blank wall:

"People of Kallendra! There is no cause for fear! Scientists tell us that the shocks will soon subside. They are the climax of the disturbances. They will

cease, people of Kallendra! Go back to your homes!
The gods will protect our great city! All will be well!"

Even as we read these words, the ground heaved
more savagely than ever, and we were deafened by
the thunders of another explosion. Then still another
crashing came from our rear, and suddenly all the
lights went out. We could hardly hear the tumult of
yells and shouts amid the far greater commotion in
the sky, but we felt the thrust of the crowd as it stam-
peded, almost knocking us over. Our plastic lamps
were torn from our hands. I could see Wulta quietly
weeping. But Lampra, lifting up her face in the illumination of a vivid lightning flash, was biting her lips
with a grim determination.

As we shouldered our way out of the public square,
the ground quaked with growing violence, and the
sky sounded more than ever like a roaring furnace.
Then the words of the Seeress of the Dawn came
again into my mind, and I understood them as never
before: "Small storms precede great! Small storms
precede great! Small storms precede great!"

Through the maze of streets between the *Romul*
and the docks, we forced a winding way, in thorough-
fares blocked by debris, or sultry red with the glow of
fires. Here and there, among houses with fronts sliced
off, looters were slinking and darting. With terrorizing
rapidity, the fires multiplied, until they glared from
dozens of points throughout the sky.

Then, as we entered one of the rare open spaces,
Langhis began pointing wildly toward Mt. Nublis.
The peak was hidden by lightning-shot clouds; but
far down the slope, a geyser of fire spouted heaven-
ward, a fan-shaped blazing fountain with a murky
crimson light.

Was it only my imagination that the air was becoming harder to breathe? My lungs were burning, my
lips and throat seemed about to crack. But pressing

181

Lampra's hand, or putting a comradely arm on Langhis' shoulders, I still kept on. The women had to be helped over the wide seams in the pavement; more than once we had to climb across piles of rubble in wanderings that seemed pointless, half-mad, before at last the lightnings and the glow of the burning city showed us the waterfront avenue, the *Cruzzo*.

Along this street, we took our way for unending distances toward Lampra's private dock. In one place, part of the avenue had fallen into the bay; in other places, we clung to walls and abutments. No ships could be seen at any of the docks. Meanwhile the fires were spreading; in places they made wide continuous sheets, from which glowing wreaths of rosy smoke curled upward.

I could see Lampra's lips opening and closing in prayer, and could almost read Uletta's words, "End of the world!" Langhis, all the while, kept on doggedly, with grim, tight-shut mouth; Wulta followed him like a faithful dog. Then, after eternities of torment, Lampra snatched at my sleeve, and by the flickering light of fires on a hill above us, I saw the tall iron fence surrounding her private dock.

While we halted with gasps of relief, she fumbled for a key. A moment later, Lampra had locked the gate from the inside and started toward the *Coral Reef*.

CHAPTER XXVII

OUT OF THE MAELSTROM

The ship rested against the dock, her portholes shining faintly. Like the *Swordfish* and the *Green Turtle*, she was virtually unsinkable when all the hatches were closed; and an internal stabilizer would keep her on an even keel.

As we rushed into the ship, we were met by Captain Arvantur and three crewmen, who hastily closed the port behind us. By the yellowish illumination of the wall strips, the Captain stood on the heaving deck, staring at us with astonishment on his red-bearded face—and who would not have been astonished at the five dishevelled members of our party?

"By Ablum, mistress," he addressed Lampra, "it's by the mercy of the gods that you found us here at all.

Every other boat in the harbor has fled. If I had had crew enough—"

Lampra and I exchanged startled glances.

"When we were done working this afternoon," the Captain hurried on, "the whole world was in such a storm we were afraid to leave."

"Can we sail at once?" asked Lampra. Staring out of a porthole, we saw a glaring river rolling down the nearest slope of Mt. Nublis.

Captain Arvantur threw up his hands in despair.

"How can we sail, mistress, with only three crewmen?"

"Count me a fourth!" I volunteered, stepping forward. "I've had experience. If necessary, I could help to navigate the ship."

"I've had some experience—also, some knowledge of the stars," put in Langhis.

The Captain reflected. "Well, with you two, I might barely make it," he decided.

"Now, Captain Arvantur—now can we sail?" demanded Lampra, anxiously.

Just then the ship heaved sharply, and struck the dock with a deep groaning sound.

Thoughtfully the captain stroked his hairy chin.

"Have we provisions enough?" Langhis gasped.

"Yes, thanks be to great Ablum!"

A few minutes later, after the men had been assigned to duty, we heard the welcome throb of the engines and were slapped by tall, strong, waves. Staring through the portholes, we saw the whole great city wrapped in flame beneath glowing smoke clouds, through which the fires of the erupting volcano still flashed. Well for us that we were locked inside, with our own oxygen generators! Rapidly the outside fumes were thickening; soon they had covered us with a heavy fog, through which we had to guide our way by instruments.

184

"You know," Langhis muttered, looking up with a worn, strained face, "if we were out there now, those vapors would poison us!"

As the darkness increased and Kallendra and the smoking volcano were blanketed out of view, we pitched and wallowed in howling wind. Hours went by; day should have arrived, but there was not the faintest brightening.

It was early morning when the culminating demonstration came. I was staring through the black vacancy of a porthole, when abruptly the blankness was pierced. From the direction of Kallendra, there came a blinding flare; all the hazes were swept away, revealing the summit of Mt. Nublis, now leagues distant. It was one great blaze of orange fire, which split apart like an exploding balloon, giving place to a gigantic cauliflower-shaped glowing cloud, which puffed out with violet, and vermilion fringes and a heart of deep scarlet that changed to a bloodshot ruddiness, then was swallowed in mud-brown and whitish steamy masses.

"Lampra! Lampra!" I cried. "Mt. Nublis has blown up!"

A minute or two later, the sound of the convulsion reached us—such a noise as, I felt sure, had been endured by no human ears before. Then, while that mighty banging and thundering continued, the father of all winds reached us. Staggering and rattling, the ship pitched, rocked, and tossed in a way no stabilizer could cope with, while the crashing of enormous masses of water was in our ears, and Lampra and I clung to one another, resolved to face our end together. To one side Langhis, struggling to keep his balance, stood trying to console the weeping Wulta.

None of us was ever quite sure if our survival was due to good luck or the expert seamanship of Captain Arvantur. We only knew that time after time, out of

185

the blackness, immense cataracts would almost submerge us. All through a day that seemed one long midnight, we fought against that raging chaos, whose fury only gradually lessened. On the second morning, there was just light enough to show us a smoky-gray overcast of ragged clouds flying above a sea of white-capped hillocks.

Then, on the shaking deck, in the yellowish illumination of the light strips, we were able for the first time to think of private matters. The haggard company, bruised and battered and with bedraggled clothes, assembled to witness an event that had been put off for long unhappy years. Captain Arvantur officiated, Wulta and Uletta stood at Lampra's side, and Langhis at my right hand, in the ceremony that at last united my beloved and myself. As I embraced her after the brief formalities, I whispered in her ear, "You were right, precious one, when you wrote me long ago that the gods would not keep us apart forever."

"I am sure," she smiled back through her tears, "the gods will make up to us for all we have suffered."

As if she had prophesied correctly, the storm passed by evening, and the stars came out in glittering brilliance. By reference to the stars, Langhis and I were able to calculate our position.

"By Ablum, is it possible we were blown so far out to sea?" marveled Captain Arvantur, when we had made our report. "So now we will head straight for Ajaka!"

"Oh, no, no," Lampra dissented. "I would never have a happy moment if we did not first return to Kallendra."

"What!" grumbled the Captain. "When you have pulled your head out of the lion's mouth, it is not wise to put it back again."

But Lampra insisted; and so did I. For more than a day, we sailed toward the capital of the Western Isles,

186

while the atmosphere darkened again, with morose banks of cindery-black mist and layers of a sulphurous dirty yellow. On the afternoon of the second day, we began scanning the horizon; no coastline, however, was visible. At first we thought that the fault lay in the heavy cloud banks and drifting layers of fog. Only when the sun was ready to set did we sight the queer triangular hill of moderate height, its sides of a dull smoldering red, smoke and steam rising from seams and fissures.

In a fascinated silence, we stood gasping and staring, the women mutely weeping. Never before in this part of the ocean had such an island been known. Captain Arvantur was the first to speak. "Great Ablum have mercy on us! There you see—all that's left of Mt. Nublis!"

As if in response, the fog came down again and the clouds deepened and darkened.

Fifteen days later, we reached the Island of Ajaka, where we were hospitably received. Langhis and I were offered posts as Associate Star Watchers at the island's Central Observatory; and there, with my friend once more my colleague, I returned to the work I loved best. Meanwhile, we found houses near each other; and Lampra and Wulta were soon the closest of friends. All would have been ideally happy had it not been for the news that gradually filtered in.

I say "gradually," for the dread rumors were not at first believed. Only after a long time were they verified. The doom that had descended on Kallendra, and on all Xandu, was no isolated catastrophe. At about the same time, a similar cataclysm struck the other four Western Isles. Also at about the same time, the four Eastern Isles were shattered and inundated. Of the great majestic city of Admenebda and all the

187

other cities of the Eastern Isles and the magnificent surrounding lands, all that remained were a few rocky islets.

The scientists of Ajaka, in commenting upon the unparalleled calamities, remarked that there had evidently been a series of faults underlying the ocean floor of Atlantis, which could not bear the tremendous strain suddenly placed upon it—the less so as many of the supposedly extinct volcanoes were actually not extinct at all, and therefore added their fires to the general disturbance. But I understood that the facts did not stop there. I could not forget that the Western Isles and the Eastern had been on the brink of war; that the war would be undeclared; and that immediate reprisals, planned in advance by both nations, would be launched in an automatic interchange that would not cease while any of the nine isles remained.

Now, remembering the long series of conflicts that began at the meetings of the *Kolem* and the hardships and torments which foreshadowed the culminating disaster, I felt greater respect than ever for the Seeress of the Dawn.

"It is true, Lampra," I said one evening, as my wife and I sat looking across the tree-covered slopes and rustic valleys of our adopted land. "Small storms do precede great!"

She looked at me out of those dark eyes that had grown deeper with wisdom and even sweeter in my sight since our union. "Yes, it is true," she answered, smiling. "But great storms sometimes precede a great peace."

www.ingramcontent.com/pod-product-compliance
Lightning Source LLC
Chambersburg PA
CBHW050734250626
47155CB00005B/1778